Victory

A Journey of Self Discovery

MARY-HELEN VICTORIA SHOMBA

ISBN: 978-1-955622-97-4

Published by

Fideli Publishing, Inc.

119 W. Morgan St.

Martinsville, IN 46151

www.FideliPublishing.com

Chapter 1

"Be sure to check online for the homework assignment because it will be due tomorrow when you walk into class. I will be available during my listed office hours so feel free to come by and ask questions when needed."

Everyone inwardly groans as Dr. King talks. Literally it is the first day of school. "Can we not at least ease into the work?"

"I agree, we barely learned anything today. What will the homework even be about?" a voice whispers to me in reply. Searching for who was talking, my eyes settle on the girl sitting behind me.

"I hope you're the only one who heard me," I mumble back. "I'm Victory, by the way."

"Victory, that's pretty. I'm Kastine Burchon, but everyone calls me Kay."

Giving her a second glance, I notice she has wavy red hair that sits right on her shoulders, complementing her circular, makeup-free face. Her green blouse brings out the green in her hazel eyes while tiny freckles sprinkle her cheeks. She seems natural, yet charming.

"Nice to meet you, Kay." I quickly turn back around, hoping class will end soon. It's not that I don't enjoy school; I just don't know how I am expected to focus when I was just dropped across the country in the middle of nowhere to attend college. I mean I know it was my choice to study engineering at a small private school, but I feel like I was caught up in the excitement of "seeing the world." I thought it would be cool to tell people I was going out of state. Now that I'm here, moving to a different state where you don't know anyone can be lonely, especially when your roommate is non-existent.

From the moment I moved into my dorm room, I knew I wasn't going to see much of my roommate Casey. My first encounter with her was also with her boyfriend Jake from back home, who she had come to college with. They were snuggled up in her bed as I returned from my first lunch on campus (I wanted to eat with her, but she wasn't in the room when I had initially come in). While still in bed, Casey introduced herself to me, asked where I was from and stuff, and I did the same, but the interaction felt weird since we were talking over snoring Jake. She told me a bit about the two of them, how they grew up together in the same hometown and have been dating since freshman year of high school, the whole spiel. Every now and then, while Casey was talking, I'd have to ask her to repeat herself when Jake would let out a serious snore. After the introductory conversation with Casey, I was debating on whether I should leave my *own* room or if I should continue to unpack when Casey said she'd be hanging out at Jake's room more, so I didn't have to deal with his snoring. *Thank God!* She also told me to feel free doing whatever I had planned to do in the room, so I just continued unpacking. About thirty minutes later, Jake woke up, Casey packed a small backpack of clothes, and the two of them left. I haven't really seen much of her since.

Okay, let's try re-focusing on the lecture. What class am I in again? Physics? I don't even know what Dr. King is talking about anymore. He seems so passionate, but all I can pay attention to are the little drops of spit flying out of his mouth. Gross! I feel sorry for the kid in front of him getting sprayed with that spittle.

Before the saliva shower gets any worse, class is dismissed. Only one more class today and then I can go rest! My dorm is literally a carbon copy of my room back home, which makes it the greatest reminder of Texas I have.

Speaking of, Texas is so much better than the Indiana in every way: the people, the cities, the vibe, everything! Although it does have one downside: the heat. I feel like if Hell were a place on Earth, Texas would be the place. With temperatures over one hundred degrees and the sun screaming at you all day, the state knows how to make its residents suffer. Maybe that's the true origin southern hospitality: since we are all melting away, we might as well do it together with artery-clogging amounts of butter and diabetes-inducing sweet tea.

The close-knit vibe among Texans rings even more true within my family. Although my dad is not in the picture (I never really knew him so he doesn't make a difference to me) and my little brother can be distant, my mom and I always have had a special connection, a connection that has only grown stronger over the years. I remember how we would always binge-watch some random Netflix show Saturday evenings, only for her to yell at me early the next morning to get ready for church (it was out of love!). I miss our random shopping excursions that always ended with a refreshing strawberry kiwi smoothie from our favorite shop down the road. I loved venting to her about my childish high school problems, like whether I should go to prom or whether I should try out for the soccer team. She was the rock of the house, the one to keep us all sane since my dad walked out. Sure, I can still call her and I definitely will, but it's obviously not the same when I am thousands of miles away.

It's also been really hard being away from Joseph. I met him at my church a few years back and our relationship had been great. Let me clear this up before you get confused because he's not who you might think he is. He's actually a 35-year-old man who happened to take me under his wing when "daddy issues" became a big deal for me in middle school. He is the one who taught me everything fathers are supposed to teach their daughters: how to ride a bike (yeah, I didn't know how until middle school, don't judge me), how to properly use a fork and knife, how to deal with bullies, how to drive ... I think you get the picture. He was like the father I never had.

Until things went south. Like further-than-Texas type of south.

You know when a girl has a guy best friend and ends up misinterpreting the friendship as something more intimate? Let's just say I know EXACTLY what that's like. Yes, Joseph was my father figure, but he was also my best friend for years. Even though I was aware of the age difference, there was still always that ungodly hope. Must I actually say it? Fine. I fell in love with Joseph. Happy? The day I learned that my childhood fantasy wouldn't come to pass occurred only a few days before Joseph got married to ... (plot twist) my mom.

You would think I would have gotten the hint when he proposed to her, right? Or after they had been dating for years? Or maybe when I first met him since he is a grown man? I guess this is where that saying, "The heart wants what it wants," comes into play.

So here I am, trying to make a fresh start and move forward, but it's harder than I imagined. I thought it would be an out-of-sight, out-of-mind type of deal, but there are things called memories that can really take a toll on you mentally.

I remember after Casey and Jake had left the dorm room that first day, how all my emotions hit me at once.

Not only did I feel lonely, but so uncertain about what my future held. The uncertainty brought an overwhelming amount of fear, so much so that I could barely catch my breath. In the past when I've gotten that overwhelmed, I'd reach out to Joseph, but he (obviously) wasn't there. No one was there, not even my own roommate.

I shake the memory of my arrival and try to relax. *It's only Monday, Victory. Let's try have a good week.* I take one large inhale, an even larger exhale, and then convince myself to put a somewhat believable smile on my face.

Chapter 2

Done with class, which means it's lunchtime! As I leave the academic buildings and head over to the cafeteria, which is in the student center, I wonder who I'm going to sit with. I have been sitting alone since I arrived on campus, but it's different today because classes have started. So many people are already in groups, talking and laughing in the lunch line. How did everyone make friends so quickly? And does it have to be so crowded? I guess I could sit alone since it's the first day of school, which makes it socially acceptable, but it is still a bit intimidating. But because I have no other options, sitting alone is the move.

"Hey Victory, over here!" I look over and see Kay waving me down. Never mind, being social is the move. *All right, Victory, put on your happy face.*

"Hey, Kay, I didn't know you had this lunch!" I exclaim. I set my plate down and get settled across from her. A gorgeous blonde girl, who is wearing an athletic shirt, sits next to Kay. I wonder if she plays a sport. I also notice she and Kay are both drinking coffee. Gross! I almost gag catching a whiff of the brewed drink. Kay notices my face and chuckles.

"I'm sorry, Kay," I laugh. "It's your coffee. I am just more of a tea person."

"You would pick tea over coffee? Like who even are you!" Kay playfully asks.

"I don't know, I just don't drink coffee. Honestly, it just smells like dirt to me."

"Well, you better believe I need my dirt every morning then!" the blonde comments. "I'm Sammie, by the way."

She puts out a beautifully manicured hand. It looks a lot better than my dry, short-nailed hands. As I reach for her hand, I can still see some dryness in the corners between each of my fingers.

"So," Sammie continues, "Did you guys hear about the party Phi Delta Theta is throwing next weekend? Word on the street is that it's supposed to be super sick and a great way to welcome the new freshman girls."

"As if," Kay snipes. She rolls her eyes as she waves off Sammie's words. "More like a way for all the Theta guys to CHECK OUT the new freshman. It doesn't sound like my scene."

A frat party? That kind of sounds like a scene I want to test the waters of. Plus being in Sammie's crowd seems like a never-ending party. I'm considering going, but for a split second I find myself thinking, *Would Joseph approve of this?* I try to shake it off, but the thought lingers.

Back in my middle school years, when Joseph and I first started getting close, he was always encouraging me to be better than I was. If I was struggling in math, he'd say something like, "You're intelligent so I know you can figure it out," or if something I tried to bake turned out disastrous, he not only ate the nasty food, but told me, "With all this practice, you'll know so many ways not to cook that eventually, you'll have to be good." It may not seem like much, but I had never had any male figure encourage me the way he did.

Growing up, the boys at school saw me as "one of the guys" because I played sports and wasn't super girly, and at my church, the guys in my grade saw me as "the bro" because I sang low in comparison to the other really pretty girls.

At the time, my mom was still fighting her own demons (being a single mom of two young kids plus bouncing from job to job ... it was tough on her) so I didn't want to stress her out, yet the boy's behavior towards me affected me in more ways than I could've ever imagined. So, when Joseph came in the picture with so much encouragement and love, all I wanted to do was show him he wasn't wrong to believe in me. I vowed to work hard to make Joseph proud of everything I did.

So what if going to this party disappoints him?

"Victory! Hello?" I see Sammie violently waving her hand in front of my face.

"I'm sorry I was thinking about something else. You were saying?"

"I was saying that I am totally going to the frat and think you should come, too. What do you say, Victory? Will you do me the honor of being my frat partner-in-crime?" I fiddle with my fingers a bit as I contemplate what to do. *I think he will be okay with me going as long as I don't do anything stupid.*

"I mean, I guess ..."

"Perfect!" Sammie squeals. Some people in the cafeteria look over at the crazy freshman making all the noise. "This weekend is going to go down in the books. What about you, Kay?"

One look at her crossed arms and you can see that she is not about it.

"Yeah, I'm going to pass on that offer, Sammie, but you guys have fun."

Sammie makes a dramatic pouty face, but then moves on to asking how our classes were. And it's at this point I'm no longer paying attention. It's funny how simple it is to act like you're listening to someone: a nod here, a chuckle there and you're good.

Just relax, Victory, it's only a party. He won't be mad at you, I reassure myself. I could just text him and ask for permission, but how immature is that?

"Everything is okay," I mumble to myself, but I am well aware that the internal battle is far from over.

Chapter 3

"Hi, Mommy, how are you?" I'm lying in my bed wrapped in my turquoise comforter. My roommate is nowhere to be seen, as usual, so I put my mom on speakerphone and get ready to listen to her soothing voice.

"I'm amazing, sweetie," she answers. "Wow, honey, you're really in college. What is it like for you? Are the people nice? Have you been to a college party? Did they offer you weed? Don't tell me you already smoked! I thought we agreed on staying away from stuff like that! I thought I at least had a few months before I'd have to have that talk and ..."

"Mom, calm down." So much for her soothing voice. "First of all, I'm not doing any drugs. Secondly, it has been good so far (lie) and the people are very welcoming (true)." What? I can't have my mom worrying about me when she can't see me anymore. "I also have not been to a college party, but I did get invited to one this weekend," I continue. "We'll see if I end up going, though."

"Well, things seem like things are going pretty good. So, what's your roommate like?"

I sort of chuckle at that question.

"Honestly, I can't tell you. I've barely seen her. We talked the first day I came in, but that same day she packed a bag of clothes and left with her boyfriend from back home. It's whatever, though. I have other people to hang with," (another lie unless you count Kay and Sammie).

I should probably be more honest with my mom, but I am trying to not be a burden. I should keep myself together for her. I pull more of my blanket over me when my phone buzzes with a notification. I get a message from ... Joseph?

A smile rises to my face as I read the message: *Hey I hope your first few days have been okay. How are you doing, kid?* My heart warms up on the inside. Oh wait, I remember I'm on the phone with my mom.

"Hey mom, I'm sorry I got quiet. I was thinking about the frat party," (I've got to stop with all this lying). "I don't know what to wear though. Would you help me find an outfit in case I decide to go? You know my wardrobe better than me so I would love some fashion advice."

"Well, you've come to the right place, my dear. Let me think. A lot of girls, especially the freshmen, will probably be wearing little to no clothing to convince the guys and themselves that they are worth a second look. You don't need to be like that. Actually, let me rephrase that: you better not be like that. Wear something that covers your body like that old, black romper you have. It's not fancy, but the shorts cover your butt so I will feel better."

"Mom, that's perfect!" I imagine myself strutting into the party. With Sammie's perfect physique next to me, we are going to be showstoppers!

Joseph texts back saying he hopes I've been enjoying my time so far. My heart skips a beat, but I know better than to tell my mom. I mean, how weird would that be? Instead, I run to my closet to try on the romper.

"The romper still looks amazing on me, Mom, even after like three years. Let me send you a picture." I snap a few pics at different angles to give her the full look.

"I just got them. You know what, I change my mind. You look too good," she jokes.

"Really?" I laugh. "This is my first college party outfit! I feel like this moment is sacred."

"It's really not that big of a deal, dear. And make sure you go with someone, please. I was a college kid once and I remember how crazy things can get and how much worse they are when you're alone.

"I know, I know." I yawn as fatigue hits me. The "excitement" of the first day of school has me worn out. Glancing at the time while stifling another yawn, I see it's only eleven, but I'm beat so I let my mom know that I'm going to sleep.

"All right, my love. Many hugs and kisses from down south. I love you and make wise decisions, dear."

"Yes, ma'am. I love you too." As I get off the phone, I also (sadly) text Joseph goodnight. This adult life is more tiring than people let on.

Chapter 4

My first Saturday morning on campus! This first week of school kind of dragged on so I'm thankful it's finally the weekend. I get out of bed to open the blinds (and find my roommate gone). Rays of sun warm my skin. It's such a beautiful day! It's eight in the morning, the perfect time to get a start on the day.

I know the cafeteria opens at eight thirty, so I quickly brush my teeth, wash my face, and change clothes, and I'm off with a book in hand to enjoy reading and eating.

As I sort of skip-walk to the cafeteria, I take in my surroundings: the birds chirping, the slight breeze. There are hardly any students walking around, probably because it's a bit early, but I like it that way. The weather is still pretty warm since it's early September, but definitely not as hot as Texas. Out of curiosity I check the temperature from back home and it's ninety-three degrees. Typical Texas. With Indiana's seventy-five-degree weather, everything seems to be just right.

As I'm walking to the cafeteria, I also notice some other cute little touches around campus. There's this flower garden filled with white, pink, and red lilies. The plaque right next to it says, "In memory of Liliane Herbert." Apparently she was an alumna who made huge contributions to the school (and not just financial ones).

The campus is also filled with beautifully large green trees that almost make you feel like you've gone camping, but with the most modern buildings surrounding you. With all the trees comes squirrels, little lizards that dart across the sidewalk, and other harmless critters. On top of that, to get to the cafeteria I get to walk past the school lake where I hear a flock of geese squawking and splashing around. The sounds of nature, as one would say, are actually pretty relaxing. It's different than the suburb I grew up in back home.

When I finally arrive in the cafeteria, there are only a few people so I get my choice of seating. I find a spot at a small table in the corner of the cafeteria and set my book down, claiming my ground. I grab a plate and fill it with eggs, a sausage link, and some yummy fruit. To top it all off, I get some OJ and happily hum some random tune on my way back to my isolated table. This is perfect: peace and quiet.

"Is someone sitting here?" I hear someone ask. Who is disturbing my peace by trying to socialize right now? I guess I shouldn't be so ridiculous, but maybe I can just keep reading and they'll get the hint. Barely glancing above the pages of my book, I mutter a quick no to whoever the guy is.

"Cool. I'm Charles by the way." He pushes his big glasses up his nose as he noisily puts his plate down and gets settled. There are so many open tables, yet he chooses to sit at the one that is a two-seater and farther than almost any other table. Great.

"I'm Victory." I say, then immediately dive into my book again. So much for peace and quiet.

"Victory, I like it. I'm assuming you're also a freshman?"

So, he's not going to stop talking. I put my book down and take a good look at this guy before answering. Obviously, the glasses are his most noticeable feature, but there are other things about him. For one, he's carrying not one but *two* textbooks, a notebook, and a calculator.

Man, it's like eight thirty in the morning. He also seems vaguely familiar, but I'm not quite sure from where.

"Yes. One week down, about a million more to go."

"It does feel like that," he replies. "I was always told that the first few months of college were the hardest. How have you been holding up?" Who even is this guy asking about my personal business?

"I'm doing great actually."

"That's awesome!" he replies. "It's definitely been an adjustment for me, but I know I will get the hang of things." There's a pause in the conversation where I'm supposed to make a comment, but don't.

"So," he starts again. "Have you started on Dr. King's second homework assignment?"

I almost choke on my OJ. "How do you know I have Dr. King?"

"Considering the fact that I sat right next to you in class all week, it was a lucky guess," he jokes.

Ouch. Well, I guess I know where I've seen him.

"I'm actually almost done with the homework, but I had a few questions on it. I was going to ask Dr. King on Monday during his office hours."

"Well, I can help you if you'd like. I had the opportunity to take Physics C in high school, so this class is more of just a refresher." He adjusts his glasses.

"I mean, uh, yeah. I wasn't planning on working on it today, but ..."

"That's okay! Where would you like to work?"

I sigh inwardly. I was hoping today would be a "me" day, but it would be stupid to not to get ahead on homework, especially when I don't have anything else to do. "I guess we can work in the student center," I say. The student center is this newly renovated building where students usually gather to do work. There are study tables and classrooms students can reserve too. Some actual classes are held in the center's classrooms, but the building is more for students. There are even vending machines and a massive flat screen in the main lobby where students can hook up their laptops and watch movies to de-stress. It's a pretty nice add-on to the campus. I guess it wouldn't be too bad to do work there. At least after this little homework session, I will have the rest of the day to myself (and then the frat party in the evening).

"Awesome. Let me just go back to my room and get my books. I'll meet you in about an hour?" He's already carrying a million and one things. Does he not already have his books?

"Sounds good ... Charles, is it?"

"Yes. I'll see you in a bit, Victory." He leaves the table with his half-eaten muffin and I just sit there for a moment. What an intrusive way to meet someone.

Chapter 5

I spot him sitting on one of the couches reading, or should I say studying, the physics textbook. He seems thoroughly engrossed by the contents as his hands fidget and his feet dance. He jots down some notes in a journal, then goes back to the book. He waves his fingers through his brown hair while his eyes dart around the page and soak in the words.

Man, this guy loves him some science.

I sit on the other end of the couch and quietly place my papers between us.

"Umm, Charles?" He jumps a little as he realizes I've arrived.

"Oh, hey, Victory! I didn't even hear you walk up."

No kidding.

He gathers his notes into the textbook, sets it beside him, and then gives me his full attention. "So what parts of the homework were you having trouble with?"

I start sifting through the assignment and hand him the paper. "I always have trouble remembering the relationship between displacement, velocity, and acceleration. Is velocity the derivative of acceleration and displacement the derivative of velocity?"

"Actually, you have it backwards. Velocity is the derivative of displacement and acceleration is the derivative of velocity."

"So, how am I supposed to remember that? Dr. King just said that was the relationship, but never really explained why."

Charles sits up a little and smiles as he begins explaining. "Well, Victory, let's think about this graphically. Whenever you have a graph and you are asked to find the derivative, what portion of the graph are you being asked to identify?"

"Isn't the slope the derivative?"

"Yes, it is! So, if I had a displacement versus time graph and I asked you for the derivative, I'd be asking for the slope, right?"

"Yes?" *Didn't I just say that?*

"Okay, well slope is also rise over run. If I look at the rise over run of a displacement versus time graph and focus on the units, I'd get meters over seconds. What is another quantity that is meters divided by seconds?"

"Umm ..." I feel like I should know this. "Oh, velocity!"

"Exactly. So that's how you can double-check which is the derivative of what. Think about the slope of a displacement versus time graph and even a velocity versus time graph. It may seem like a lot to do in the beginning, but eventually you'll do it so much, you'll end up remembering the relationship off the top of your head."

"That actually makes sense." I scan the problems I was struggling with and realize that they don't seem too bad when anymore. "I'm going to try to finish the rest of the problems on this page, Charles. I have another question on the next page, but I'll ask you about that in a bit."

"Cool. I have some calc homework I'll be working on, but feel free to ask me for help at any time."

He pulls out his calculator and goes to work. I continue working through the problems to make sure I actually do understand what is going on.

Let's see, I think. *I've been given a velocity equation and the problem is asking for the acceleration at t=3. Well, the slope of a velocity versus time graph would have the unit meters per second per second, or meters per second squared. Those are the units for acceleration! So, if I find the derivative of this velocity equation, I'll have an equation for acceleration. At that point it's easy. I just plug in 3 for my variable t and then I'll have the acceleration at 3 seconds.*

I turn to the next page and realize it's just more iterations of this same concept. This page deals more with integrals, but I can figure it out. While I'm in between problems, I occasionally look over at Charles and watch how he murmurs his thought process aloud. It's kind of weird.

As I finish up my homework, Charles is still working on his. "Hey, Charles, I'm going to head out since I'm finished, but thank you for your help. I probably wouldn't have gotten this done today."

"No problem, I'm happy to help anytime. I'll see you around!"

"See you."

Well, that went better than I expected it to. With physics out of the way, I feel a lot freer. I wonder what Kay's doing today. I know the frat party is this evening, but it would be cool to do something with her beforehand. I'm feeling extra social so I call her, hoping she'll respond.

"Hey. Victory!" She's probably so surprised I actually contacted her.

"Hey, Kay, how are you doing?"

"I'm great, just enjoying the day. I'm actually about to head out and do some last-minute swimsuit shopping. You know ALL the suits are going to be on sale now that summer is basically over. I always find some sweet deals!"

Although she isn't wrong, I still find it a little weird since summer is over.

"Do you want to come with me?" she asks.

For some odd reason, I actually do. I mean, I'm not doing much today anyways.

"Sure, why not?"

Chapter 6

"Ooo, look at that scarf! It's so cute! Do you see the matching gloves? And that beanie! What a chic outfit!" Kay's eyes are dancing all around the store. She didn't strike me as one to care about clothes, but she definitely seems to be enjoying herself.

"Didn't we come for bathing suits?"

"Oh, yeah, you're right. Let's go check out that clearance rack over there." I kind of laugh on the inside because we are already in an outlet mall and nearly everything is on sale. Maneuvering through the store, Kay and I are surrounded by a combination of warm winter clothes and cheap summer stuff. Obviously, the store's trying to get rid of their leftovers. A beautiful brown-haired salesperson sees us wandering around and makes her way over.

"Hi, ladies! May I help you with anything?"

"No," I start. "We are just ..."

"Yes, of course!" Kay exclaims. "We are looking for cute bathing suits that scream 'summer is here,' but that aren't too over the top. Do you happen to have anything left in stock?"

I'm still trying to figure out what that description means when the salesperson exclaims, "Oh I totally get you! Come right this way and I'll show you some of our most summer-vibish suits!"

Kay excitedly follows while I low-key drag my feet across the floor. I'm kind of starting to regret coming. Kay's nice, but I could be on my computer, watching a movie or searching conspiracies. (It's a secret hobby of mine. Ever heard of the reptilian theory about our world leaders? Yeah, it's pretty wild; look it up). Or I could have been drawing another picture to add to my one-color collection. It's a montage of multiple pictures I've drawn that all have one color shaded in each. Eventually I want to have the entire rainbow and ...

"Victory!" Kay laughingly yells. "I've called your name like three times! You seem to space out a lot."

She's already caught on? You know something is a problem when someone you barely know points it out to you.

"I'm really sorry, Kay! What were you saying?"

"What do you think of this bathing suit?" She shows me a vibrant yellow, lime green, and pink bikini with a fringe all over the place. It's ... interesting.

"Umm, I think I need to see it on you."

"All right. While I try on mine, you can try this on!" She shows me a super-cute baby blue and navy two-piece that has high-waist shorts and a high neckline. "I don't know, it just seems like it would look really good on you," she comments.

That was actually really nice of her.

"Thanks! Let's go try them on," I reply as my mood lightens.

Approaching the dressing room, I'm kind of nervous because I've always been slightly wary of looking at my body in mirrors. It's not like I'm fat, but I'm not stick thin. I'm just kind of there, you know?

"Okay, Victory. Are you ready to show me?"

"Yeah, uh sure." I walk out grudgingly and show Kay the suit.

"Oh, my goodness! Victory, you look good! The suit hugs you in all the right places! I didn't know you had such an hourglass."

As I turn to really look at my body, I see that she's right. I *do* look good.

"I don't really like what I'm wearing," Kay comments. "It's too much."

Back to reality, I see Kay frowning at the lemon suit. "We can look for something else!" I say consolingly.

"Yes, please!"

After a little more searching, Kay ends up buying a green bikini that matches her eyes and I buy the high-waist cutie. We return to campus just in time for dinner, which we end up eating together, and honestly, it was nice. By the time we've returned to our own residence halls, I'm feeling like I actually have a friend. Yeah, it's a shock to me, too. On cloud nine, I start getting ready for the frat party. Tonight's going to be amazing!

Chapter 7

It's almost time to go, so Sammie adds her final layers of mascara before we head out of the door. She looks cute with her high-waisted shorts and crop top. A pair of worn-down Converse tops off her I'm-cute-but-don't-have-to-try look.

"All right. I am ready to go. How do I look, Victory?"

"Stunning!"

"Thanks, girl, now let's go!"

Walking outside, we are hit with a bit of chilly air since the sun has gone down. Nonetheless the night feels young and full of promise.

"You know, Sammie, I never really went to parties in high school," I confess. Sammie halts mid-step with her mouth gaped open as she puts her hand on her forehead for extra effect. I'm starting to learn that this girl is super dramatic.

"Oh my goodness! You've never lived," she exaggerates. "The parties I went to were always lit. At least the ones I can remember were."

"Sammie!"

"What? Your girl has to live a little. And plus, what good is a party when you CAN remember everything? That's no party I want to be going to!"

"Ha-ha, I guess." We continue walking side-by-side and I notice other groups of people are heading in the same direction. "Looks like we aren't the only ones planning on having a good time."

"Oh, girl," Sammie explains, "we are going to have *more* than a good time. We're going to have the time of our lives!"

The music is pounding in my chest and people are going crazy! I see people letting loose, girls twerking for random guys, people playing beer pong in the back. Everything is taking place in the basement of the frat house, so there are only dirty walls, sticky floors, flashy lights, and enough drinks to last a lifetime. I always saw this in the movies, but here it is in real life. Honestly, the energy is exhilarating!

"Here you go. I brought us some drinks!" Sammie hands me a mysterious concoction in a classic red Solo cup. Without hesitation she downs her drink and begins swaying to the music. Some guy comes up behind her and holds her hips while they move. I look at Sammie's face and can tell she's in her element, like she doesn't have a care in the world.

I try matching her moves, but can't seem to find the rhythm. *All right, Victory, this is your first college party. Live it up, as Sammie says.* I slosh my drink around a bit ... and look for the nearest trash can to dump it. I can live it up without being smashed. Maneuvering through the maze of bodies, I end up finding a trash can outside where the air is dense from smoke.

"Hey, you want to play beer pong?" There's this cute guy with a drink in one hand and his cockiness in the other. You can tell he knows he's beautiful and it's slightly annoying. Beer pong sounds like fun, but unlike Sammie, I actually want to remember this party.

"Why don't you play it with your ego? Looks like he's always ready to dish it out with you."

He just laughs as he mumbles, "Freshmen." I watch him walk up to another crowd of people whose faces light up after he asks them the same thing. They all walk over to play with him.

What's going on with you, Victory? You're supposed to be having fun. It's supposed to be the night to remember, the official start of your college life!

I contemplate going back to the arrogant guy, but decide to keep my dignity. I definitely won't smoke, mainly because my mom would kill me, but also because I'm not feeling it. I could go back to the dance floor, but for some reason that idea doesn't sit right with me either.

Frustration begins to build up in me. Why won't I just do something, anything, out of the ordinary? Maybe I should just call it a night. There will be other parties anyways. I decide to find Sammie and let her know I'm leaving. As I walk back inside, I wonder if she's still dancing with the same guy. Yup, she's still grinding.

"Hey, Sammie, I'm going to head out."

"Whaat?" She slurs. "Da nigh isil yung!"

She doesn't look good. How much did she have to drink?

"Are you okay?" I ask. I pull her away from her "dance partner" so she can see that I'm serious. "Do you need me to walk you home?"

"Noo. I fine! Kay's come." I call Kay to make sure she really is coming. When she says she is, I drag Sammie outside and wait with her. It felt like we were only inside for a few minutes! Sammie and I sit on the concrete steps right outside the house. The steps pretty cold on my legs, not to mention the slight breeze that sends chills down my spine. I watch a few cars pull up, but none of them stop in front of us. Finally, after what feels like forever, a little black smart car stops in front of us. I kind of chuckle at the sight of it.

"Kay, thank God you were you available to pick Sammie up. I have no idea what Sammie drank, but she doesn't seem well."

Kay takes one look at Sammie and stifles a chuckle. "Yeah, I can see that. Will you help me bring her to my car? I can give you a ride back to your place, too, if you would like."

"That would be awesome."

We manage to get almost-dead Sammie into Kay's tiny car. Maybe someone messed with her drink. Once Sammie's strapped in, Kay exhales. The brief ride back to our residence halls are in silence. Kay obviously got out of bed to pick us up and seems as though she's still there mentally. Sammie's passed out and boy is she going to feel it in the morning. I just continue to stew in my annoyance.

Kay parks her car and we drag Sammie safely into bed after she's had some water. Thankfully she doesn't throw up, but that could be a morning battle. Afterwards, Kay drops me off to my room where I find my roommate dozing off. At least she's in the room! I don't know if we'll ever have another decent conversation though.

As I get into bed, I think about my "exciting night." So much for the night to remember. Maybe I should at least have taken a sip of something. Or maybe I should've danced. I didn't necessarily have to dance on anyone. Whatever. I'm done thinking about this.

I'm about to go to sleep when my phone lights up with a message. From Joseph. I see that he sent the message hours ago, but with the terrible Wi-Fi on campus, I just now get it. He says he's just checking up on me and my heart skips a beat again. At least there's a little light at the end of this depressing night I've had.

Chapter 8

Well, the weekend's over and the second week of classes are underway. The gears are really rolling now as professors assign a lot more homework and clubs and extracurricular activities begin meeting regularly.

I am just trying my best to ignore my emotions and keep up with all that's going on, but as I walk through the halls, I see so many posters for different activities. "Cupcake club!" one flyer reads. "Want to Learn to Tango?" another asks. I see yoga classes, history appreciation club, choir practice and all sorts of other things! I know I need to do something outside of school, but where do I even start?

I'm about to avoid all of it and leave the academic buildings when one flyer catches my eyes. "UNASHAMED," it says in all caps. *Unashamed of what,* I wonder. Looking up closer, I see it's a Christian Bible study that meets every week. Skimming more of the flyer, I see that the first meeting is tonight. Hmm, this seems interesting.

Back home, I was always in church. I went every Sunday and Wednesday, helped out in the Children's Ministry, went to almost all of the youth events, you name it! I was like the poster child, the one other kids wanted to be like and the one parents wished their kids were like.

Being seemingly perfect on the outside did have its downfalls, believe it or not. It was a very isolating state to be in. People didn't want to be around someone who never showed their shortcomings. However, the sight of anything less than perfect would have some people I knew rejoicing, so I always made sure to never give that crowd the satisfaction. Consequently, when I battled with my identity in middle school, on whether or not I was supposed to be male or female, not many people knew. When I contemplated suicide after a really bad breakup, I definitely kept that low-key. When I fell in love with my mother's husband…

I think you get the picture.

What I have learned over the years is that keeping your struggles a secret to appear tough is the STUPIDIST thing one could do. So, maybe surrounding myself with other Christians will help me get the right perspective. *If I start on my calc homework now, I'll have more free time in the evening for the meeting ...*

Well, it looks like I'm going. One extracurricular activity down, about a million more to go. I'd say I'm doing pretty well!

Chapter 9

I don't know what I was expecting when I walked into the classroom where Bible study is being held, but it was definitely not a room full of people. I see so many new faces!

There's this guy with a super awesome Afro, another girl with really pretty brown curls, some other person with big glasses sliding down his nose ... Wait, I know those glasses: Charles. It's a surprise to see him here, but since he's the only one I remotely know, I grab a seat near him. He looks a bit startled to see me, but in a good way.

"Victory, hey! What a pleasant surprise."

"Hey, Charles. Big turnout, huh?" I say as I motion to the bustling crowd of students around us. There are so many conversations going on I can hardly hear myself think.

"It appears so. I didn't know you were religious."

"I don't think I would consider myself religious, since that's more of the rules instead of the relationship, but I did grow up in church."

"Yeah I feel like I'm the same way. I still go to church pretty regularly too. So, how have you been doing?"

"I'm not going to lie, I have been feeling a little overwhelmed lately with classes and stuff, but I'm glad I stumbled on the 'UNASHAMED' flyer. It was kind of hard not to miss it honestly."

"What, the neon yellow flyer didn't blend in with the other posters?"

"You know, surprisingly not," I laugh.

"Hello, everyone!"

The booming voice comes from the front of the room. A tall, built man with a brown man bun has gotten everyone's attention. He has the largest smile on his face, as if this is the only place he wants to be. I wonder if anyone else notices that little freckle he has on his right cheek. His demeanor gives off a chill vibe, probably because of the relaxed sweatpants and hoody look he's got going on. My guess is that he's the leader of this organization.

"Thanks for coming out to the first UNASHAMED meeting of the school year. I know things are getting crazy in school now so I really appreciate all of you guys showing up. My name is Josh and I am the current president of UNASHAMED." Bingo, guessed it. "I'm a senior studying mechanical engineering. Shout out to all the MEs in the room!"

A few people hoot and holler, including Charles. I just sit quietly in my seat while observing all that's going on.

"So here is a quick rundown of how things are done here. First of all, we usually start with a game to ease the mood and get people mingling. After that, we'll have the Bible lesson, whether that be reading the Word, watching a video, etc. Next, we'll discuss what we've just learned, take prayer requests and then close out. Any questions so far?"

A few people shift in their chairs, but no one asks anything. "If not, let's get on with this game. Here's a rhetorical question for you guys: how well do you trust each other? I need teams of two, with one person blindfolded."

I barely glance over at Charles to find him blatantly staring at me. "I'll be blindfolded," I say. "My sense of orientation is amazing."

"Well, I'll be the judge of that," he comments. He grabs a washed-out red bandana from the box Josh brings out.

I am slightly disgusted, but swallow my pride. After all blindfolds are put on, Josh continues.

"All right, blindfolded people, your job is to listen to your seeing guide and allow them to lead you through this maze I'm currently making."

I hear chairs squeaking and tables groaning across the ceramic floors.

"Now make sure you're not peeking under the cloth and you actually listen to your partners. They're the ones that can see, not you."

"Did you hear that, Victory?"

"Oh shut up, Charles."

"Oh. and did I mention the catch?" Josh continues. "My seeing friends can't talk. They can only guide with one hand."

I feel one of Charles' hand slip into mine as he gently pulls me towards the start of the maze. I am very startled, but how weird would things be if I say something now?

Josh begins timing us. Charles walks me through some tight spaces between (what I assume are) desks, on top of some chairs, and all the while I'm thinking, *this guy is holding my hand*. I couldn't tell him not to because it was literally in the directions of the game, but I can't help but wonder what is going on in Charles' mind. He is a nerdy type of cute, I guess. *No Victory, you're still trying to get over everything. You can't handle another person right now.* But do guys usually just hold peoples' hands like that?

When I hear Josh yell "time," I quickly pull my hand out of Charles' hand and yank the blind fold off. "I'd say you were a subpar guide, Charles," I say as I find my seat.

"It wasn't my fault you didn't trust me," he counters.

I find myself wondering if he's just talking about the game.

Chapter 10

It's a typical Thursday night after classes and I am hanging out in Kay's room. We are both preparing for this physics quiz we have tomorrow while also enjoying each other's company (that's code for we-really-aren't-doing-anything-but-love-convincing-ourselves-we-are). Kay puts on some music and I immediately recognize the piano melody from the introduction. It's "10,000 Reasons" by Matt Redman, one of my favorite worship songs from church back in Texas!

"Do you go to church, Kay?" I ask her.

"Yes, ma'am, every Sunday. I am still trying to find a place to settle down, but there are a couple of good ones around campus."

If anyone needs to go to church, it's me. Hashtag, number one sinner right here. Plus, it would be pretty cool to have a church-buddy, you know someone to explore the options with. Considering I'll be in the Midwest for at least the next four years, I probably should find something solid now. *God, I pray the plans You have for me do not involve me actually living in the Midwest after college.*

"You should come with me, if you want to. It would be nice to have some company on Sundays," Kay offers.

"Of course I will! I am glad to have met another church-goer besides Char," but I fade out before finishing the sentence. Charles. He's a nice tutor, but what if he really likes me? I don't know what it's like to have another guy like me. Plus, I'm still trying to get over things with Joseph (but am I really trying?). At the same time, shouldn't I see what else is out there? I can't just say no to everyone that comes in my direction. Similarly, I shouldn't say yes to everyone, either. Maybe I can talk to Kay about it. I mean, I need someone to help me process what's going on and which feelings are right to be having. But how weird is this entire situation? Can I really just tell someone?

"Kay, may I ask you something, or maybe, tell you something? But if you're trying to study or something, it's fine. I can just talk to you later. We can actually talk on the weekend or ..."

"Victory, what's going on?"

"I'm a little bit conflicted. I just, you know what? Let me tell you a story. So once upon a time, I liked this guy from back home for years and we hung out a lot, but he never felt the way I did and it's been weird being so far away and then yesterday I went to the Bible study and Charles' held my hand and ..."

"Slow down ,Victory. What's the deal this guy from back home? And who held your hand yesterday?"

"He was just this person, but I don't know, it was just a long time ago so I should be over it and stuff, but I'm still struggling at times,"

"Victory, speak coherent thoughts. And I want the uncut version, not the sugar-coated version you're trying to vomit on me."

Oh goodness, what do I say? Why did I even bring this up? She's going to think I am a freak. I mean, how many times do you hear about someone falling in love with their mom's husband?

Even though everything in me was screaming no, the thought of having someone else to talk to besides myself was so intriguing, I began spilling the beans, and then the whole can, and then next thing you know, I've literally told Kay everything, even my little tidbit about Charles. As I'm finishing up, my heart races as I study her face to gauge what type of judgement she's going to throw in my direction.

"Wow, Victory, you've been holding onto a lot on your own. I'm grateful that you were willing to open up to me. I hope you're feeling better after sharing?"

I didn't want to admit it, but I did feel significantly lighter. It's crazy what opening up can do.

"I do feel a lot better, but that doesn't change the situation at hand though, you know? I'm still in love with my stepdad, Charles might be crushing on me, and I have this constant guilt weighing on me for the way I feel. Not to mention, I still have little meltdowns concerning everything. How will I ever recover? How will I ever be able to move on? If things ever progress with Charles, how on earth would I be able to admit this to him? I feel like I'm too broken to ever be loved by someone else."

"I hear you, Victory, I really do, but I'm afraid you're wrong. Your stepdad was there for you in ways your real father never was and it's human nature to want to cling onto that special type of love. You shouldn't feel guilty about it, but just understand that at some point you're going to have to allow yourself to move forward. Charles crushing on you is a good thing, too! But it kind of seems like you don't want to let yourself like another guy, maybe because it's mentally disloyal to your stepdad?"

Can someone tell me why Kay is literally piercing my heart with her words? The Holy Spirit doesn't play games, man.

"Umm," I start. "In times of sadness, I definitely vowed not to be with anyone else. No one compares to the first, you know."

"No one compares to anyone because everyone is unique. You shouldn't be comparing people. And how do you know there isn't someone out there who will be better than you've ever imagined? I believe God has so much good planned for you; you just have to be willing to receive it, even if the goodness doesn't look like the picture you've painted in your head."

As I ponder on Kay's words, I begin to realize the truth behind what she's saying. At this point in my life, I need to choose to move forward. Easier said than done, am I right? As "10,000 Reasons" plays in the background on repeat for the millionth time, I feel the desire to "bless the Lord" and "worship His Holy name" for speaking to me in an unexpected way. Maybe if I made a conscious decision to move forward, I'd find myself moving in that direction. I feel arms wrap around me and look up to find Kay hugging me.

"I love you, Victory."

Those simple four words are enough to make me cry like a baby for the next hour.

Chapter 11

"All right class, hand in your homework," Dr. King says.

I smile at Charles as he hands me the stack of homework. "Thank you again," I mouth to him.

"You're welcome," he whispers back.

Ever since he helped me the first time (and Kay's inspirational speech), the tutoring sessions just continued. I mean, Charles is a great teacher and I could use all the help I could get!

"Now, today we are going to quickly revisit displacement, velocity, and acceleration before moving onto our next topic. I hope you guys actually did your homework because in order to check your understanding, we have a quiz! And yes, it was on the calendar." The entire class groans, except for Charles and me. I look over at him and give him a miniature thumbs up. He smiles back.

"Students keep your eyes on your own paper and no calculators. When you finish, bring your quiz to the front." I get my quiz and immediately start working. The problems are similar to the ones from the homework. *The following equation represents the deceleration of a bullet.* It only takes me five minutes to finish the five problems. A quick review of my answers and I turn in my paper.

"Ten minutes class."

I glance around the room and see most people are still furiously writing. My guess, it's the third question that's stumping people. I think Dr. King purposely threw in a curve ball with that one. Looking to my left, I see that Charles is also done and has resorted to reviewing his notes from Friday's class. Of course he is.

"Students, you have five minutes."

Some students really start shifting in their seats. I hear violent erasing in the back of the room while someone else lets out a heavy sigh. I take a look at Kay behind me whose eyebrows are furrowed. Her eyes bore into the paper as if the answer is written in invisible ink.

"Two minutes."

People start getting up and turning in their quizzes. As Kay stands, she looks troubled but nonetheless turns in her quiz. Before the two minutes are up, everyone has turned in their work. Dr. King, who has had time to grade a few papers, makes his way to the front of the classroom.

"Enough with the quiz business. Let's learn some more physics, shall we?"

"That was a breeze!" Charles laughed.

"Yeah, I know. It felt good to actually know what to do! Plus, I'm done with classes for the week so I'm on cloud nine!"

"You could say that again!" Charles answers. "Hey, do you want to eat at that little café across campus? They have amazing potato soup!"

"Well, lucky for you, I'm in the potato soup mood." My phone vibrates and I see I have two messages. *Joseph?* No, from Kay and my mom. Kay's wondering where I'm at and I tell her I'm eating with Charles. Mom wants to know why I haven't called her in forever and I feel kind of bad.

"What's with the frown, Victory?"

"Oh, sorry. It's just that I haven't talked to my mom in ages and now I feel like the world's worst daughter."

"You aren't the world's worst daughter. Just call her or set up a time to. It's normal. I forget to call home, too."

"Yeah, you're right. On another note: why don't we get the food to go and get a head start on physics homework instead?"

"Why do I feel like you're using me?" he jokingly asks.

"Because I am ."

Charles' face hardens.

"Relax, man, I'm only half-joking. You're also pretty chill, too."

He relaxes his face a bit, but there's still a slight strain. "I guess we can get the food to go then."

"Perfect! Potato soup, here we come."

Chapter 12

We arrive and the place is packed. Although the line is super short, we obviously are the last stragglers from the lunch rush.

"Where did all of these people come from? Do we even go to school with this many people?" Charles asks. I'm literally asking myself the same questions.

"I have no idea, but good thing we are getting our food to go. So, where should we eat?"

"How about we take a break from work and relax in my room for a little bit? I mean, it's Friday!"

Relax? Does Charles even know what that means? Plus, in a boy's room? Isn't that like, I don't know, code for sex or something? Is that what college guys do nowadays – bribe girls with food? I am not going to lie, that is pretty smart, but kind of terrible, honestly. I'd rather have guys tell me up front what they want then to hide their true intentions. I literally feel like I'm about to throw up.

"Oh, look, Victory, the food is ready!" He picks up both of our meals and walks over to me with a mischievous, sex-filled grin. "Do you want to invite your friend from our physics class, too? It would be fun if we all hung out and got to know each other better."

Oh. So I may have overdramatized things just a tad bit. I tend to do that. A lot.

"Of course I'll invite her over. Her name is Kay by the way."

"Kay, I like it. Not as much as I like Victory, though," he kindly says.

I knew it. He does want sex. I text Kay so fast to make sure he and I don't hang out long enough for anything to happen. *I'm already walking towards his room,* she replies. Thank God for trustworthy friends!

"I heard that was a good movie," Kay points out. We are devouring our food while "relaxing" on Charles' bed with his laptop in front of all of us. I'm in between Charles and Kay and I am not going to lie, I am a little nervous with Charles hairy leg brushing up against mine. At least he and I aren't the only ones on the bed.

"I did hear that The Perfect Date was decent, but it's also a super chick flick," Charles adds. "As much as I love making sure my guests are happy, I would prefer not to watch that. What about, this animal planet documentary?"

Of course, Charles would suggest that. It literally takes everything in me not to roll my eyes at him. Kay giggles next to me as if she knows what I'm thinking.

"Jeez Victory," Charles continues. "I hope you know that you have a terrible poker face and that I am joking. I definitely would not watch that with you guys. I'm saving it for myself for later."

"Oh, so you have jokes, Charles?" I snipe. "I don't know you had time for that with all the studying you do."

"You're complaining about me studying, but yet you're always asking me for help? Is there something ironic about this situation?"

Kay just smirks at me as I sit there wondering where this comedic Charles came from. He's really starting to come out of his shell and I kind of like it.

"Can we just watch the cheesy movie, please?" I ask. And with that, Charles leans across me and presses the spacebar to start it. When he re-positions himself, his fingers accidently lay on top of mine. He doesn't move them. I don't move my hand either.

Chapter 13

I think I'm going to call Joseph. It's normal for a daughter to call her stepdad, right? Hmm, but is that really a good idea? The last time I heard his voice I was fighting tears as I walked towards the check-in line at the airport on my way here. Am I even emotionally stable enough for that? Why do I always overthink things with him?

Let me put this into perspective: think about the first person who truly made you feel like you were worth something. Think about the first person who truly saw you for you, the first person you fell in love with. Think about the first person who you told all of your silly secrets to without receiving judgement, the first person who held you and comforted you when no one was around. Think about the first person who saw you for who you were becoming, not just for who you were. Were some of those different people for you? For me, that was all encompassed in Joseph. Now don't get me wrong, my mom definitely helped in so many ways, but as a young girl, it somehow resonated differently from a man.

So, what's the real issue then? It's not like he's disappeared or is out of my life. Well, for the last five years of my life I lived alongside this person, did so much with this person, and now it's like I've been ripped away from my other half. A bit melodramatic, I'm sure, yet it's the truth. My emotions are probably also being magnified because of my "daddy issues." They say growing up without a father figure can be detrimental and sometimes I feel like I can see the consequences of that reality in my life.

You know, I did tell Joseph about my feelings awhile back. When they first started brewing, I had felt so guilty I spilled the beans. His reaction? He told me he understood my perspective given what I had been through and would never stop be the FATHER figure I needed in my life. It was so comforting at the moment, but in this moment all I want is to be held by that same father figure. I call him.

"Hi, Joseph."

"Victory, how are you?"

So many things run through my head, but all I say is, "Good."

It's just after dinner and I'm watching Netflix in my room. Well, I guess I was until I called Joseph. The day had been amazing after hanging out with Charles and Kay. Charles and I ended up leaving Kay's room after the cheesy chick flick when her mom called her. Charles then walked me back to my room and that was that. Such a chill Friday, until I decided to call Joseph.

You know I can't really explain why I decided to call him. Maybe it's because back home we talked every day, but that hasn't been the case since school started. Maybe it's because I was feeling forgotten. Or maybe I just missed him.

"That's amazing to hear," Joseph says. "Your mom was telling me you and her finally got around to talking, but I happened to be at the store picking up some groceries so I missed the call. Update me on what's new."

So many things run through my head, but all I say is, "The usual."

"It's your first year of college so I don't know what 'the usual' means for you yet. Give me details, sweetheart."

So many things run through my head, but all I say is, "You know." There's a moment of silence. I can tell that this conversation is going to end in tears.

"What's going on, Victory? Did something happen? Do you want me to bring your mother?"

"NO!" I kind of yell. "I'm fine." But it's kind of crazy because in reality I'm not. Just earlier today I was basically holding hands with Charles, yet the instant I start talking with Joseph my emotions go awry.

"I, I. It's just hard sometimes, you know?" I kind of explain. "I'm trying to make friends and enjoy college," I try to continue. "And don't get me wrong, Joseph, I am having fun, but I miss being home. I miss Mom and I actually kind of miss my little brother, too. If I'm completely honest, I really, really miss you. I guess I just got so used to having you around that I forgot what it was like before you stepped into the picture. And the guys here are different than you. They're kind of weird and super, super nerdy."

"Wait a minute, guys? Is this your way of telling me that there is someone in the picture?"

I think about Charles again. As kind and surprisingly funny he is, he would not be able to handle me. I'm too emotional. I'm too needy. Let's face it: I'm just too much, period.

"Well, that's not what I'm trying to say, but I don't know if this one guy likes me, and I kind of like him, but he's so different than you and I don't know if I should even be thinking about guys right now and basically I really want to go home."

There is a bit of silence on the other end as Joseph kindly lets me attempt to calm myself. Along with my word vomit comes the tears that were waiting to come ever since I dialed his number.

"Victory, I know what this is really about and it's okay. And you also know that your mother and I have spoken about this and she also completely understands."

My heart nearly drops to my stomach with those words. For some reason I thought he (and even more so my mom) would've experienced some type of memory loss and forgotten everything. Plus, I still feel too embarrassed to even try talk to my mom about it.

"I know the move has been hard and transitioning to a completely different way of life has probably been tough, but you are stronger than you know. I'm sure you're hurting, but don't hold onto the negativity for too long. At some point you will have to choose to move forward and enjoy this new season of life God has brought you into. I am always here with open ears to help you in this transition and will keep praying for you, but I don't want to see you miss out on all of the good that is coming your way. You deserve to enjoy college and your life."

I'm sniffling while trying to listen to his words. I know he's right, but I want things to be the way they were. Will the good God has for my future compare to the good I had in the past? I'm sure it will, but as of right now I'm not trying to find out. Point blank. I listen to Joseph say a few more comforting words, I act like I'm good, and then hang up. Then I cry some more.

Chapter 14

The chirping birds wake me on this "fine" Saturday morning, but I just kind of lay in my bed for a while. My stomach growls a few times, but I don't feel like moving. I don't want to do anything. After talking to Joseph yesterday, I decided to cool it with Charles. Charles is too nerdy for me and I'm too extra for him.

My new goal is just to get through college so I can go back home. Yes, I mean go back home to Texas where Joseph is. It's obviously too difficult for me to be away, so I'll just do my best to get back. I wonder how all of that would play out, but that's not something I'm trying to think about right now.

You know, I never realized a college bed could be so comfortable. I would have continued to lay in bed, but my growling stomach can no longer take it. I throw on tights and a big shirt, grab my slides and head out the door.

"Thank you," the lady says as I scan my ID. There's Chinese food today (yum) so I grab a plate and just lay on the fried rice and orange chicken. Also if I'm honest, the relationship I have with food is like no other. Food is always there for me, which is why I usually have to be careful with how much I eat. Yes, I am definitely one of those people who will eat just to feel better. Usually I try my best to monitor the amount I eat, but today I kind of don't care.

As I approach the end of the line, I see fortune cookies! I grab three and head to my little corner in the cafeteria. I'm half-expecting Charles to pop out of nowhere again like he did the first day we met, but when I'm left unbothered for a few minutes, I know no one is going to be talking to me anytime soon.

I've only taken a few bites of my fried rice when I decide to crack open my first fortune cookie. It reads, "Treasure the ones who have been brought alongside your journey." My mind immediately goes to Charles. My mind also wonders over to Kay. She's been nothing but amazing towards me, even with everything she knows about me. Kay's probably one of the only people I truly consider a friend. I guess I could talk to her, since I'm in a bit of a mood. Nah, I'll let myself relish in it for a bit.

After finishing my meal, I go back to my room to start on some homework. I have physics homework I could start. We are currently learning about rotational kinematics, a topic I felt pretty good about until torque got introduced into the mix. *You could call Charles,* I think. There's no way I'm calling Charles right now. I'll start on calculus and leave physics for tomorrow.

I open my calculus textbook and find the assigned problems. I am grateful we were assigned the odd-numbered questions, since the answers to those questions are in the back of the book. I'll at least be able to double check my answers. It's always nice to know whether you did a problem the right way before you do an entire assignment wrong.

I remember I still have two fortune cookies left so I crack one of them open. Pulling out the little piece of paper, I read, "Sometimes your blessings are behind the wall of your perspective."

Wow, that's deep. If that's not God trying to speak to me, I don't know what is. I sigh knowing that I'm not going to be able to get far on my homework if I don't sort out my little mood. Grudgingly I set my work off to the side and kneel down by my bed to pray. I can act like the only reason why I'm praying is because I want to get homework done, but honestly I this inner desire to let go of my bitterness.

"God, I hear you. Thank you for being so kind to continue trying to speak to me. I know I'm being extra and I'm sorry for that. May you forgive me for being angry with you, Joseph, myself, and basically the world. I'm still frustrated that I found myself in the position I am in with Joseph. I have to choose to let go of the past and move forward, but I don't want to. I'm angry that I always think about him. I'm angry that I can't like another guy without comparing him to Joseph. I'm angry that I'm angry. I'm also tired of being angry. I'm just so tired of holding everything in and living this lonely life."

As a natural moment of silence unveils itself, I'm reminded of my first fortune cookie, about treasuring the ones alongside my journey. "God, thank you for blessing me with Kay. She heard my drama and didn't judge me. It's nice to know that I'm not a total freak to everyone. With this in mind, may you help me forget about my past and move towards the blessings you have for me? Thank you once again God. You're awesome."

When I get up off of my knees, I feel a lot lighter. My mind is clear and I'm ready to tackle not only this calculus, but my perspective as well. Does that mean I'm going to run towards Charles? No, I'm still going to keep some healthy distance from him until I really figure out how to deal with myself.

Oh, I still have one more fortune cookie. Based on these other two, I'm really curious to see what this last one is going to say. I quickly break open the last cookie. "Pop the pimple you can't stand to see." That's disgusting. What does that even mean and why is it in a fortune cookie? I chuckle at the thought of a pimple-popping joke inside of something people eat. Okay, I'll stop. At least it was humoring, I guess!

Chapter 15

"I'm excited you're coming to church with me, Victory! I think you're going to like this one, too."

I'm sitting in Kay's passenger seat while she's driving us to Gospel Way Ministries.

"I visited this church last week and I really enjoyed it!" she continues. "People worship so freely. It's amazing."

Well, that's perfect because right now, I need to get back into the swing of things with God. She pulls into the parking lot and it's packed. We're keeping our eyes open, but we can't seem to find an open space. Kay's literally driving down every aisle with no luck.

While looking around, I'm thinking about this new-found desire to actually obey God for once. I'm really feeling church this morning. I can already tell it's going to be a powerful service! My spirit is open and ready to hear what God has to say!

Kay finally finds a remote spot in the cafeteria's equivalent to the deserts of Sahara and we quickly get out and jog in, since we are pretty late. As soon as we walk through the door, I feel the presence of God. It's like a peace that quiets even the slightest restlessness I have in my heart. For the first time in a long time, I feel genuine joy.

Kay leads us to two seats that are surprisingly close to the front of auditorium. The worship team is singing out praises to God, worshiping Him for being their hope, their joy, their reason for living and the words seep deep within me. I begin to pour out my frustration and bitterness in the form of adoration, allowing myself to get lost in God's love again. I'm hesitant at first, but quickly get all in. I forgot about how amazing it was to be in God's presence. He's so good. He's too good.

As the worship portion ends and the message begins, the attitude of worship doesn't end. People are actively participating in the preaching, jumping up when they feel a revelation, shouting amen when they're ceasing a promise from God. It's infectious! I find myself waving my hand in the air too while saying, "Preach pastor," not to follow people, but because there's liberation in agreeing with a word from God.

After the service, I am feeling rejuvenated. I am reminded of the promises of God and the fact that He has so much good in store for me. Even when I see Charles approach, I don't feel an ounce of negativity. I see Kay look over at me to gauge my reaction, but I greet Charles like there's nothing going on, probably because there isn't anything going on.

"Hey, Charles!" I say. "I didn't know you came to this church."

"I didn't know you guys came either. It's nice to see familiar faces. Maybe we could carpool on Sundays to save gas," he half-jokingly asks.

"That's actually a really good idea," I chime in. I look over at Kay and notice she's trying to mask the confusion she feels. It's probably because the other day I told her about how I didn't want to deal with Charles anymore. Now here I am, being so happy-go-lucky. God has that effect on people.

Kay's phone goes off. She picks it up, and as she listens to the call, a concerned look washes over her face. She starts consoling whoever is on the other line, saying she'll be right there. Charles and I kind of stand awkwardly, waiting to hear what's going on. When she hangs up, Kay explains that Sammie woke up at a frat house and needs a ride back to campus.

"Sammie is just a little spooked because she had a lot to drink last night and so I am going to pick her up."

I hope Sammie is okay. I shoot up a quick prayer on her behalf.

"Something has happened like this before and knowing her, she's not going to want anyone to see her in that condition," Kay explains. "Victory, do you mind going back to campus with Charles?"

A slight hesitation comes over me as I realize what's going on, however, I don't want to lose the "Jesus high" I'm on so I brush it off and agree to go.

"Thank you so much, Victory. You're awesome!"

We hug and then I watch her race off.

"So," Charles starts. "Shall we?"

Instead of being awkward, I play along and say, "Yes sir, we shall."

We head to his car and a uncomfortable silence fill the space between us. I'm wondering if he can he tell I haven't been calling him as much. Has he gotten the vibe that I've been trying to stay away from him?

Well, if he has, he doesn't give much of an indication. In fact, the uncomfortable silence quickly comes to an end and it's as if we never even stopped talking. He dives into this stupid story about how he bruised his finger while trying to make himself a peanut butter and jelly sandwich and I can't contain my laughter!

"I'm telling you, Victory, crunchy peanut butter is deadly. If I had not been trying to flick the stray peanut off of the counter, I would have never flicked the corner of the counter, thus avoiding all bruising. One has to wonder why there was even a stray peanut to begin with."

"Charles, I think the real question is, why didn't you just get a paper towel and pick up the stray peanut?"

"Victory, stop with the extra inquiry. That is neither needed nor the source of the problem here. The root issue is the chunky peanut butter."

"Stop, Charles!" I laugh. "My belly literally can't take it anymore."

I'm still laughing as we pull up to some train tracks. We are stopped by an oncoming train. Charles puts his car in park as we wait the train out. I'm finally catching my breath from laughing so hard when I realize Charles is just staring at me.

"What is it, Charles? Was my laugh too obnoxious for you?" I joke. But his mind seems to be elsewhere.

"Victory, I don't mean to make you uncomfortable, but what's been up? I feel like you're trying to avoid me. If it's something I'm doing, at least let me know so I can stop?"

My face freezes up. I'm completely caught off guard by Charles' bluntness and my inability to discreetly keep distance from people. I need to get better at that. Or maybe I shouldn't be trying to perfect a skill like that? That's a mental conversation for another day. I gather my composure, look up at this long train that now seems never-ending, then meet Charles' gaze.

"Charles, I ..."

"Wait," he interjects. "Before you say anything, I need to say this before I chicken out again. I like you, Victory. I mean I really like you. When I first saw you sitting by yourself in the cafeteria I thought to myself, 'That's the really pretty girl from my physics class.' And you were all by yourself so I thought it was a great opportunity. We starting hanging out and I learned how goofy you can be when you aren't so deep into your thoughts. I know we don't know each other very well yet, but I want to get to know you. I think you're beautiful from the inside out."

The train clears out and cars are now moving again. I'm sitting there in silence while Charles puts his car in drive and moves forward. He periodically looks over at me, then after about a minute keeps his eyes on the road. I'm trying to form words, but nothing comes out. I try to muster up cohesive thoughts, but nothing surfaces. How on Earth am I supposed to respond to that?

"Charles," I start. "I don't know what to say." I think back to when Kay, Charles, and I watched a movie in Charles' room and how I started developing feelings for him. I also think back to the sadness I had felt after I talked to Joseph on the phone. A part of me kind of wants to see what could be with Charles, but another part of me wants to hold onto the first man to ever show me love. Is it possible for me to actually be with someone else or will I always be condemning the other person for not being Joseph? There is no way I'm telling Charles all of this, so I decide to give him the watered down version of the truth.

"I'm sorry I've been quiet for so long, I just had to figure out my feelings. Honestly, Charles, when we first started hanging out I just saw you as a good tutor. Then we started spending more time together and I learned that you were more than just a studious nerd. I started developing feelings for you.

"However, I still have some stuff from back home that I need to work out before I get into any relationship. I'm not ready for anything."

Charles pulls into campus and parks in front of my residence hall. I'm getting my stuff together, ready to leave when Charles asks me to hold on.

"I don't know if you misunderstood me, but I don't want a relationship yet, either. Victory, I just want to get to know you. Yes, eventually I would like to be with you but that doesn't need to be on the table right now if you don't want it to be. You are worth the wait."

And then my heart just melts. I'm what? Worth the wait? This guy barely even knows me and he is already so certain. It's comforting and nerve-wracking all at the same time. I've been completely myself around him so at least I know he isn't into some façade I've put on. It doesn't hurt to get to know someone on a deeper level, plus the baby feelings are still there.

"So does mean we're like 'talking'?" I ask him. What? Can you blame me for wanting clarification?

"If that's what you want," he answers. Is it really that simple? So Charles and I are talking. I did not expect that to happen when I woke up this morning. As I gather my stuff together, he comes over to my side of the car and opens the door for me. I step out and he closes the door behind me.

"Um, one more thing. Do you want to go out on a date, maybe this evening?"

"All right, Charles." I catch his smile widen before he tries to play it cool. After a quick (and slightly awkward) hug, I head to my room. When I arrive, I drop all my stuff, lay on my bed, then replay the last twenty minutes of my life in my head at least a hundred times. So I'm talking to a guy. What the heck? Who would've seen that coming? I guess I'm kind of excited.

Man, Kay is going to get a kick out of this.

Chapter 16

Not only does she get a kick out of it, she literally falls to the ground when I tell her about how Charles asked me on a date. Or maybe she just fell over all the clothes I have laid out. Whatever the case, she's flipping out!

"Wait a minute, so he actually said, 'I think you're beautiful from the inside out?' And then you decided to start 'talking' to him? Does he know about the stuff from back home?"

"No, I haven't told him that stuff. We've literally been talking for like an hour, why would I bring that up already?"

"You don't want to hide something like that from him and have him find out later on. He'd be hurt that you weren't honest from the beginning."

I kick around some of my clothes. Why does Kay open her mouth sometimes? I definitely do NOT want to talk about Joseph to Charles, even if she has a point. Now I know this is going to be on my mind during the date. Ugh!

"Think about this, Kay: If I'm trying to move forward from my past, why should I bring it up again? Don't you think I should leave the past in the past?" Try to answer that, Kay! In my head, I've already stumped her with this question. I mean, I should be looking forward right?

"Well," Kay begins, "You need to be honest about your past because it shaped who you are today. In order for Charles to truly get to know you, he needs to know what things you have gone through that have made you, you. And if we're honest, some of your past struggles are also your current struggles too."

Mike drop. I hate this girl.

"Okay, okay, I hear you, Kay. Can we cut the sappy talk for a bit so I can find an outfit to wear?"

"I am one step ahead of you."

She pulls out an off-the-shoulder maroon dress that hits right above my knees. It's flowy, simple, and cute! I put it up against my body and do a little happy twirl.

"Kay, I am saying yes to the dress!" We both laugh, while we clean up my mess. I've littered the room with stuff. It's kind of crazy that I'm acting like this, considering the fact that not too long ago I was ignoring Charles. What's even more crazy is that once I'm ready and the room's clean, I start getting nervous. Am I really about to go on a date with Charles? What the heck am I doing? What if it's weird? What if Charles tries to hold my hand? What if he tries to kiss me?

"Victory!" Kay shouts.

I come back to reality.

"You need to breathe, okay? You have fear written all over your face. If you aren't ready to do this, you don't have to."

I really contemplate blowing Charles off, but decide to stick it out. I want to prove to myself and Joseph that I can actually do this.

"I'm good, Kay. I've decided I'm going to just have fun tonight."

"Good. If you end up needing me, I'm only a text or phone call away. And, you have got to tell me all about it when you get back!" My phone lights up with a text from Charles saying he's outside. I take a few deep breaths, hug Kay, think about how cute I look, then head out the door.

Breathe, Victory, breathe. It's just a date. You're okay. Actually, you're better than okay. You're great. I'm still mumbling to myself when I turn a corner and immediately see Charles' car and him sitting in the driver's seat. Our eyes lock and he breaks into a cute, little grin. He gets out of the car to open the door for me.

"Wow. You look more amazing than you usually do," Charles says as I get in his car. He shuts the door behind me then hops back in the driver seat.

"Thanks, Charles. You look pretty good yourself. So, where to?"

I'd be lying if I said Charles just looks pretty good. He's looking like eye candy right about now! Although he still has his nerdy glasses, he traded his usual sweat pants look to some nice pants and a button down. I can smell his aftershave and it has a nice scent. He cleans up nicely. I'm impressed.

"I've got a surprise for you," is all he says. I'm tempted to protest, but just decide to let it be. Usually I don't like surprises, so hopefully this one doesn't throw me off.

We listen to some Chris Tomlin while casually talking about how our days are going. The weather is literally perfect, in the mid 60s and there's a nice breeze. The windows are slightly rolled down and it feels so nice. I'd love to just sit outside and take it all in! I close my eyes and enjoy the peaceful mood.

"You falling asleep on me?" Charles asks.

"No, of course not. Just enjoying the moment."

"Well, I hate to ruin your mood, but we're already here."

My eyes pop open to see the big surprise. I'm kind of confused as I look around and see a playground for like two-year olds. There are a couple of old, raggedy benches next to the unstable-looking slide and I'm trying to figure what on earth he's thinking.

Charles opens my door and actually turns his back towards the janky slide. I'm still looking at the rust on the bench when he calls my name. I turn around and finally understand why we're here.

Across the parking lot is the most beautiful field of flowers I have ever seen. There's a walking path where I see an old couple holding hands and talking. There's a cute bridge that leads the walkway into some really pretty trees. I hear the trunk of the car close and see Charles with a picnic basket and a blanket.

"You ready?" he asks.

I smile as I grab the playfully grab the blanket from him and start walking towards the field. I plant myself in the middle of a bunch of beautiful white daisies.

"Charles, this is amazing. Literally in the car I was thinking about how I wanted to be outside taking in the beautiful weather."

"Yeah, I checked the weather and when I saw it was going to be in the 60s, I knew we had to be outside. I have sandwiches, some fruit, and water, so help yourself."

Charles takes the food and kindly lays the blanket on the grass before setting the basket down and laying out the food. In between bites I ask him about his family and find out that both his parents work in the medical field. His dad is a doctor and his mom is a nurse (a little scandal, his mom used to be his dad's nurse). He has one older sibling, a sister, who followed in his mother's footsteps of nursing.

"She's now married and living in Washington with her husband," he adds. "They've been out there for two years now. We're all just waiting for the 'I'm pregnant' phone call."

"That would be exciting, wouldn't it? Being an uncle?"

"Oh, of course! I'm excited for the family to grow since it's always just been me and my sister. So, tell me about your family back in Texas."

I choke on the water I'm sipping. I think about my "family," my biological father who is non-existent, my stepfather who I'm actually in love with, my younger brother who doesn't associate with me, and my actually amazing mother who I've struggled to let into my personal life because of my stepfather. All these thoughts run through my head as I'm coughing profusely, trying to clear this water out of my airway.

"Are you okay, Victory?" Charles has run over to me and is now patting my back profusely. I heard one time that patting one's back doesn't actually help when someone's choking, but it seems to help me as I calm down. I'm only calm for a moment until I remember what Kay said to me before I left. Tell Charles the truth about my family? I can't do that. He'll think I'm a freak! Maybe I am one, but he doesn't need to know that yet. My heart starts racing, my breath speeds up and my emotions are out of control.

Oh no, I'm having one of my "swings." I need to get out of here. I can't let Charles see me like this. I'm about to get up and leave when I feel a hand gently rubbing my back. Charles. I forgot he was still right next to me. He probably heard my intense breathing. Great.

"Victory, we don't have to talk about your family. Obviously there is some hurt with that. Today is a beautiful day so let's make the most of it, okay?"

I just nod and sink into his arms. He hugs me and his embrace is comforting. It's really nice, actually. For now at least.

Chapter 17

Since our first date, Charles and I have hung out a lot more. It's been nice just getting to know him and let me tell you, Charles is a character. Outwardly he's nerdy and goofy, but his heart is so big. He truly cares about the people close to him and it shows in his actions. I really like him!

Lately though, I've been feeling like Charles wants to be more, like make it an official thing. He's been dropping hints by saying things like, "You and I are so good together," or talking about "our future" and I don't quite know what to make of it.

I wanted to talk to Kay about it, but she's been caught up with homework and hasn't had time to listen to me rant. A huge part of me longs to call my mom. I feel like these are the types of things daughters are supposed to talk to their mothers about. Honestly, I just want to tell my mom everything. I'm tired of carrying this weight. I've been feeling like I've just had so much in my head that I'm going to literally going to implode! I need to do something, anything to stop myself from thinking so much. What can I do?

When I was younger, I took piano lessons. They weren't anything fancy, just enough to learn some chords and some keys. I haven't played in so long though! I remember a few songs I taught myself, too. There is a piano on the first floor of my residence hall, so I head there to play. It's like seven in the morning on a Tuesday (my first class isn't until ten) and the floor is empty. Perfect.

Why am I up so early? I just wake up early sometimes. My fingers rest on the white keys and I start playing a few chord progressions. I'm a little choppy at first, but the more I get into it, the smoother the playing becomes. I start adding in other chords, playing in other octaves, dancing up and down the keyboard. I used to do this all the time. I used to just play and play until every negative emotion was emptied from my heart. I would play every gospel song I knew to remind myself that there was hope in God. As I play now, I'm feeling lighter, freer, happier.

I'm no longer at school. My spirit is elsewhere, worshipping God for who He is.

"You play really well."

I immediately release the keys and feel the door to my emotions close up again.

"I didn't mean for you to stop. Would you keep playing?"

I turn around to see a student who looks to be around my age watching me intently. I still haven't said anything, considering the fact that I'm just now returning mentally from wherever I was.

She continues trying to fill the silence with her words. "I'm Elishea. I've seen you around campus before, too. You really do play well. What was that you were playing?"

I'm still lacking words, so I simply nod and start getting up to leave.

"Please don't leave!" she asks.

"No, it's okay. I was just leaving anyways," I respond. Why is it so hard to get some privacy at this school?

"Okay, well, I'll see you around," Elishea exclaims. "What was your name again?"

"Victory," I mumble.

"Victory. What a beautiful name!"

Chapter 18

Charles and I are heading to lunch after physics class and I know something is going to go down. How do I know this? Could it be because Charles didn't want to eat in the cafeteria, but wanted to take the food to go and eat in my room? Or maybe because he said, "Victory I think you and I need to talk."

I have been dreading this conversation because I still haven't figured out where I am with everything. Or maybe the issue is I know where I am and I know that it's not where Charles is at. I just need to be honest and tell him the truth, that I'm just not ready.

We walk into my room and he gets settled at my desk. My physics book is still out and I find myself reminiscing on how we first met in the cafeteria, or I guess how Charles met me. I sit on my bed, not even wanting to touch my food. Charles takes a few bites, looks at me, then stops. He knows that I know that he knows what's about to go down.

"Victory, I think it's time we talk. I don't know about you, but I have really enjoyed getting to know you these past two months. I know that I want to be committed to getting to know you and helping you become the woman God has called you to be."

As usual, I have no words. I just stare at him, then awkwardly look into the distance (aka at the ground next to him).

"Victory, say something, please? What's going on in your mind?"

What's going on in my mind? Charles, I'm thinking about you. I'm thinking about how amazing you are, how you're so silly, but cute at the same time. I'm thinking about how you make me laugh and how you care so much. I'm thinking about how much you're working on yourself to get closer to God. I'm thinking about the fact that I actually like you and am starting to actually care about you.

But on the flip side, Charles, you know what I'm thinking about? Joseph. I'm thinking about how he was my first love. I'm thinking about how he showed me what it meant to be loved, cared for, held, important for the first time in my life. You're not him. I've been struggling to not compare the two of you this whole time and just the thought of all the work it'll take to let go of the past frightens me. I'm not ready for a relationship. I'm not ready to commit. I know that's what you want, but I can't. So, you know what I tell him?

"I think I'm ready. I really do like you and even though this is my first relationship and there are some nerves, I trust you. I want to see where this goes."

The brightest smile illuminates on Charles's face and I almost feel happy on the inside. I almost believe myself. I almost believe this is what I really want. But like a mirror with a small crack in its surface, there's something slightly off about this image.

Charles is hugging me now, but all I feel is regret. Maybe I will grow into this. Maybe if I really focus on getting to know Charles, things will work out. I'll actually learn to be ready to commit and then this will just be part of a huge testimony. Yeah, that's how it will go.

I plaster a smile on my face and hug Charles back. My first real relationship. Fleeting thoughts about telling Charles about Joseph come to mind again, however, I push them away. My heart is divided, but what else is new? Maybe I was just meant to live a life like this.

Chapter 19

Word about Charles and me spreads like a wildfire. Random people I barely know ask me about us. "Is it true, Victory? How did that even happen? When did that happen? Charles is so into his schoolwork, I never thought he was looking for a girlfriend." With everyone's inquiry and my divided heart, the amount of tension I have built up inside of me is unreal: piano time.

The last time I played the piano I was nicely, yet still annoyingly interrupted, but I've learned my lesson. Before playing I thoroughly search the area to make sure that Elishea girl isn't going to be popping in. I am not in the mood to talk to her or anyone else for that matter.

It seems like the coast is clear, so I sit on the old, brown piano bench and start playing. I begin playing some simple chord progressions, then transition to some of the songs I've taught myself. I'm no Beethoven, but it's nice to play gospel songs with the little bit I do know. Something about gospel songs always just brings an immense amount of peace. I'm really getting into it now as I close my eyes and allow my body to sway a bit when I hear slight cough in the distance. I open one eye expecting to see Elishea, but to my relief see some random person walking past. I start up again.

"Wow, you're back at it again! Your playing is still as beautiful as the last time."

My fingers leave the keys as quick as frustration fills my heart. What is with this girl? What is with the people at this school? Do they not know when to leave someone alone?

"Hello ... Elishea." It takes everything in me to not tell her off. "How are you," I grit through my teeth.

"Oh, I'm fine, thanks for asking. Today was a bit stressful at work because, well, you've seen those workers at the cafeteria. They're crazy! If I told you some of the drama that went down with them, you'd be shocked. And some of them just have no respect for other people's privacy, you know what I mean?"

I didn't realize she worked here. I just assumed she went to school here, too.

"Yes. I know exactly what you mean."

"Hey, Victory, are you coming?" Kay asks.

She walks up to the piano in her pajamas and I remember that tonight was our movie night! We planned to reminisce about the good old days by watching *High School Musical*. Kay and I are fanatics! I literally know the words to every single song. Some of my frustration starts dissipating as I realize how much I needed this girl's night.

"Going where?" Elishea asks.

None of your ...

"Victory and I were going to watch *High School Musical*. It's one of our favorite childhood movies so you better believe we're about to sings our hearts out!"

"*High School Musical?* I love that movie, too!"

Kay replies, "Isn't it amazing? You should join us if you don't have anything else to do. I'm Kay, by the way. What is your name?"

I watch the two of the exchange names and numbers and I think to myself, why? They begin chatting it up and I just pack up my stuff. Why do people ruin things?

Chapter 20

"We're all in this together! And it shows, when we stand, hand in hand, make our dreams come true!"

We are all belting the final song of the movie and it's quite a scene. We ended up going to the student center to watch the movie because of the big flat screen (and it's open all night, which is also pretty nice). To our surprise, there are still other students working even though it's past one in the morning. Talk about dedication!

Elishea and I are dancing on the dark brown, wooden table in front of the TV while Kay is using her water bottle as a microphone, just swaying to the music. Elishea is actually a really good singer and became my singing buddy from the first song. I sing Troy Bolton's part, since my voice is lower, and she just kills Gabriella Montez's vocals. The last note plays and with that, the credits are playing. We're all laughing, out of breath, low-key sweaty, but having a good time (thank God the other working students have headphones in). A part of me doesn't want this Tuesday night to end. I can't remember the last time I felt so carefree.

"We should definitely do something like this again in the near future. This was a lot of fun!" Kay says.

Elishea and I both nod in agreement while picking up all of our belongings. Kay has to walk in the opposite direction of Elishea and me, so she heads out, while we continue together.

I'm wondering if this is going to be awkward, but it actually isn't. Elishea just asks me where I'm from, what brought me here, and other things students usually talk about when they meet for the first time on campus. We end up sitting down back by the same piano we were at before the movie, and since we are still talking, we take a seat.

Elishea asks me about my home life and since we've bonded by singing over my favorite childhood movie, I find myself wanting to talk. I open up to her about everything, from my dad not being there when I was younger, to falling in love with Joseph and everything in between. She just sits there and listens.

After my story, she says, "Wow, you've been through so much."

I don't know why those words shock me so much, but they do. I always viewed myself as the guilty, shameful daughter who didn't deserve anything but seeing that someone else, someone who doesn't really know me doesn't see me that way is huge. I think I really like Elishea.

I end my story by talking about how God's been helping me through everything, but in the back of my mind I know I haven't really been letting Him. I want to take the spotlight off me for a while, so I ask Elishea what her story is. She talks of a toxic home life that was filled with poverty, hostility, and abuse. And she thinks I've been through a lot?

That evening Elishea and I stay up talking until five in the morning. At three in the morning, we were so hungry our stomachs were talking louder than we were! We ended grabbing some chips and chocolate from one of the vending machines down the hall and walked back to the piano. Once four rolled around, we went back to my room (honestly because I wanted to be wrapped up in my warm blanket), but still continued talking. I don't know what it is, but there's something that draws me to her. Plus, it's nice to have another genuine friend. By the time we parted ways, I already knew I had met a sister for life.

Chapter 21

I dedicate this Wednesday morning to work on a project that's due ... tomorrow. It's for my college prep class, which is basically an easy A so it's obviously at the bottom of my to-do list. The whole premise of the project is to set goals for ourselves and then creatively present them in a PowerPoint. The goals can be academic, personal, spiritual, whatever we decide. The minimum requirement is three, but your girl here wants to go above and beyond, so I guess the first question is, what are my goals?

I know academically I want to stay around a 4.0. I know that's kind of a stretch for an engineering degree, especially since basically everyone I know from back home says engineering is hard, but if feel like I set my academic goal high then maybe I'll achieve more than expected. Now, what do I want personally for myself? I mean I guess I want to be better than I was yesterday, but what does that even mean? How do I quantify that? I don't want to gain that freshman fifteen, that's for sure. I'm definitely not putting that down, though.

I start really thinking about my life, my first few weeks of college. It would be nice to expand my group of Christian friends, even outside of Charles, Kay, and Elishea. In high school I was a part of the youth group, which had over thirty kids all trying to live for God. It was a really amazing environment because I felt like I could unwind and share life with a whole army of people. Granted, I never told them how I felt about my step-dad, but the hardest that situation has ever been is now, so I never felt the need to. Ever since coming to college, I've digressed and have gotten more wound up than ever. The thought of not feeling so wound up all the time is almost intoxicating but seems too good to be true. With everything concerning my stepdad constantly weighing on my shoulders and Charles not knowing anything about it, I don't know another way to live but wound up. And even if Charles did know, what would that change? My embarrassing secret would be out so I guess that would change. Yet, I'm still not over the guilt and disappointment of all of it and that fact is the root of a lot of the tension I feel between Charles and I. Maybe he can't feel it, but I can.

Anyways.

Back to my project. Man, I really need to get a hold of myself mentally. I go off on tangents way too often. So, I have what, one goal? All right, let's skip the personal goals for now and focus more on spiritual goals. I know I want to go to church every week so that's something I could jot down. Oh, maybe another social goal is to join at least one organization. I know freshmen were advised not to do too much this year since we are still trying to figure out the swing of things, however, one shouldn't be too much. Maybe I can keep going to that UNASHAMED group. I don't know though, we'll see. Well, that's three goals. Now I'll just make my PowerPoint presentation extra beautiful.

Chapter 22

"And my last goal is to get a hamster. It's definitely flushable, I think?"

We all laugh at that last goal. That was some girl named Sophia King who took this assignment with a grain of salt. The only factual thing she said was that her pet had to be flushable. No, I'm not lying. If you want a pet on campus, the size requirement is that it's flushable. Gotta love college.

A guy volunteers to go next and his goals are typical: get good grades by maintaining such and such GPA, stay in shape by working out three times a week, etc. It was a solid presentation, though. After he sits down there's a bit of silence as we wait to see whose man enough to go next. I decide to just get it over with and get up.

After hooking up the projector's HDMI cord to my laptop, I smile at the photo I chose for the first slide of my presentation. It's of me and Kay when we first went shopping for bathing suits. I remember after that day Kay and I just clicked and it's been smooth sailing since. Kind of. I guess it's smooth sailing when she's not giving me advice.

"Good afternoon, class. My name is Victory and I would like to share with you all some of the goals I have for this school year." I switch to the next slide that has a picture of my planner and all the daily tasks I write in it.

"My first goal is to maintain a 4.0 GPA." The looks on peoples' face after I stated that goal was interesting. "My reasoning behind this is that if I set the goal high, then I'll most likely land higher than if I set, what some would call, a more reasonable goal." People's faces relaxed a bit, but still seemed skeptical. I just continued talking.

"My next goal is to go to church every Sunday." The next picture is of me, Kay, and Charles from this past Sunday. I stare at Charles' face for a second longer before I continue talking. "I have a small group of people I go with so it will help keep me accountable."

Proceeding to the next and final slide, I stare at a picture of me with my family. I feel like I haven't talked to them in forever. The picture was from when my mom,

Joseph, my little brother, and I went to the beach for a family vacation. Joseph had picked my mom up and she was screaming while laughing. My little brother and I had just buried ourselves in the sand and were covered in it. We were making fun of each other, but actually having fun. It's one of the few times I remember the entire family being happy. At that moment I had even forgotten about the situation with Joseph. A part of me wonders, if I can forget about it for a moment, could I forget about it altogether one day? Maybe the whole situation doesn't have to dictate so much, you know. I mean it didn't for a moment. Maybe I can try to extend that moment into longer moments. Eventually one moment could become one day, then a week, a month, a year. Next thing you know, I don't even really care about what happened anymore.

What a concept!

I finish presenting my last goal, which is to talk to my family at least once a week, then spend the rest of class contemplating what my life could be like if all of this was in the past. I also think about how it's time for me to be open with Charles. And if it's too much for him to handle, then it probably wasn't meant to be anyways. It's probably best to do it sooner rather than later too. I sneak a text and ask him if he can make some time for me to talk to him this evening after dinner. Of course, he says yes and says he can't wait. He also sends heart eyes. I would have never believed this guy was such a softie. I just pray this blows over well.

Chapter 23

Charles and I end up having dinner together at the cafeteria. It was actually really good, too! We were both just laughing about stupid stuff, talking about anything and everything under the sun. We went from talking about how I used to love Sponge-Bob SquarePants to how flare jeans are not okay. We even talked about how mascara is really bat poop (it's kind of weird that we willingly applying bat poop on our eyes, if really you think about it). We leave dinner holding hands and it's an amazing feeling. I almost forget we're about to have one of the deepest talks known to man. Almost.

The walk over to his room is nice, too. The sun has already set and the air is cool, so I lean up against Charles' arm to feel some of his warmth. He leans his head over mine. While things between us seem good at this moment, I can't help but wonder how he's going to react to everything I tell him. He's probably thinking I want to, I don't know, confess my love to him or something. Not even close. Or I guess it is, but I'm confessing my love to someone else.

The closer we get to his room, the more nervous I get. He'll understand, won't he? But I know deep down that's not my biggest concern. The issue I have is that with all I have going on, I can barely be in this relationship without drowning under the weight of myself. And why has Charles fallen so hard? Why couldn't things have just gone slower?

We arrive at his room. Fun fact, we almost never hang out in his room because his roommate is super dirty, and he gets embarrassed. He's already looking for another roommate for next year and we're barely towards the end of the FIRST quarter. The only reason we're here is because my roommate is actually in the room (huge shock) so he talked his roommate into letting us have a few hours.

I go sit on his bed and he sits at his desk. He turns his chair so that he's facing me, giving me his undivided attention. Chills run through my arms, so I use his blanket to cover myself up. I wonder if it's the nerves.

"Well, Victory, I'm listening to you. What's going on?"

I want to be honest, but I need some encouragement or motivation, something. I think back to when Charles briefly told me about his past. He told me he only had one ex-girlfriend, but never really went into detail about her. If he's willing to tell me about her, then I'll be ready to talk about my past.

"Remember when you told me you had an ex-girlfriend, Jessie? You've never really told me the details about what happened with her and I'm curious. It's important for us to be completely honest with each other, and it will me open up if I know what happened with you and her."

The smile he had on his face immediately goes away. I know that relationship hurt him deeply and even talking about it is hard for him.

"What do you want to know?"

"Everything. I want to know what happened between the two of you."

He buries his head into his hands and deeply sighs. I let the silence draw on since I know he's trying to muster up courage. You and me both, man.

"Victory, I'm not proud of what I've done. Honestly, I don't want to tell you anything and it's not because I want to hide things from you, but because I'm ashamed. I'm trying to be better with you, though."

"I know that, but the way you are now is partly because of your past. In order for me to understand you now, I need to know what you've been through and what has shaped you." As I finish that inspirational statement, I feel like I should plaster the word "hypocrite" across my forehead. It's funny how much easier it is to point out someone else's shortcomings versus of your own. *Why am I like this*, I ask myself?

Charles looks off into the distance and has trouble meeting my gaze, but I can tell he's about to start.

"My ex and I dated for three years. We got together sophomore year of high school and then broke up this past summer before coming to college. We went to the same high school and had some classes together, but really met in math club, Mu Alpha Theta. I know it sounds cheesy, but that's when I first noticed her. She was the president, bossing around a bunch of nerdy boys and one girl who always showed up late to meetings, if she showed up at all.

"One time after a meeting, I stayed behind to help arrange the classroom we'd been using and we found ourselves just talking. She was a lot nicer when no one was around. Behind her bossy persona was another soft nerd who just wanted to be the best she could be. We exchanged numbers that night and were dating in the next two weeks.

"Things were so good at first, but as time progressed, she began bossing me around. If I didn't do things her way, it was the wrong way and no matter what I did, it was wrong. It was impossible to please her."

He paused for a bit, and it seemed he was lost in all of the memories flooding back to his mind. He slightly shook his head, as if trying to forget all that he was remembering.

"Do you know I've never completely opened up about what happened with her to anyone?"

"I know. I'm grateful, really."

He shifts in his seat again and clasps his hands together before continuing. "So, one night we had been arguing about something I had done to upset her. I was trying to apologize, but she wasn't listening. I walked over to her to give her a hug because that was all I could do sometimes to calm her down. Then she, well, she started kissing me and of course I kissed her back."

He stops again and won't meet my gaze. I can tell he's wondering about how I view him, but there's genuinely no judgment on my end.

"I mean, it's not like we hadn't kissed before, but you know, one thing led to another and we found ourselves in a bad position, worse than we had ever been in. It was about to be one step too far, but her dad just happened to come back and saw us on the living room couch. It was wild because of all the nights we had hung out alone at her parent's house, it just so happened to be the night things were escalating that her dad showed up. We were scrambling to cover ourselves, pick up our clothes and stuff, but it was too late. Jessie was crying, her dad was yelling, and I got my things and ran out of the house as quickly as I could. I didn't know what else to do at that point, you know?

"The next day I called her and apologized for everything, told her I didn't mean to let things get that far. Thank God He spared me from going all the way, but it might as well have been. I also ended up telling her that I couldn't be in a relationship with her anymore. I couldn't take the constant degrading and the impurity within the relationship.

"At the time I had really been searching for God and asking for His guidance and the relationship felt like a weight that was bringing me down. Although I felt at peace with the decision, it was hard to end it with her. She cried so much, promised she would be better but I had heard all of those words before. At that point it had been two years and ten months. After hearing her cry though, I decided to try to stick it out and see if anything would change. We had just been through so much and I wanted to make sure I had done everything I could to make it work.

"After that conversation things were fine for like a week before she went back to constantly being upset with me, yet still wanting physical love from me. I really couldn't take it at that point and finally called it quits.

"She was so upset that she started telling her friends intimate details about me, about things we had done together to her friends and other people at school. It was humiliating because I was supposed to be the goody-two-shoes Christian boy. Many people thought she was stretching the truth, but it was the truth. I'm not proud of that relationship and I feel like a lot of it is my fault."

Charles pauses and finally looks into my eyes like he's trying to read my expression.

"Victory?"

I look straight into his eyes and with every genuine bone in me I say, "Charles, I want you to know that I'm not judging you at all. In fact, I've heard worse stories in my life, believe it or not. You telling me about Jessie doesn't change the way I view you. It honestly makes me respect you even more since you were willing to tell me about it. Thank you, really."

He still seems a little shaken up, but better. Dang. He really did open up. Which means it's my turn.

"I have something I want to tell you, too."

He looks up at me and I can tell he's studying my face. I try to play it off but at this point I am a nervous wreck and it's written all over me. Charles comes to sit next to me and holds my hand.

"Charles, I need to tell you about my family."

Chapter 24

I just start talking. I literally, actually just start talking. And I don't stop, either. I start from the beginning, too, of how my real dad wasn't in the picture and how Joseph stepped in. I admit how at first, I was hesitant with Joseph, but then ended up learning to appreciate him ... an appreciation that went too far. I just say everything because at this point, what else should I do?

I don't really focus on Charles' face but allow myself to immerse myself in this trip down memory lane. I feel him tighten his grip around my hands and I find myself wondering if it's because he's tensed up or because he's trying to comfort me. Maybe it's both? As I finish, I slowly look up and to try to read his expression. His face is blank. He doesn't even say anything.

"Um, Charles. Aren't you going to say what you think?"

"I don't really think anything to be honest. I'm not one to let someone's past be an indicator of who they are now. If I'm frank with you, Victory, I love you and I don't care about what you have going on or what's happened in your past. All I know is that I've never felt this way about anyone before and I want to continue growing what we have."

Did he just? No, he didn't. Love? How can he love me? Does he really know? No words. I have no words. How does Charles always manage to be so, persuasive? I don't think that's the right word, but I don't know how else to describe it. Here I was thinking, maybe after telling Charles the full truth, he'll see that I'm not ready for a relationship.

What does he do instead? He admits to me that he loves me. I can't tell him I'm not ready now. That's going to crush him. And it's not like there aren't feelings there on my end: they are there, but I still need to choose to move forward and I haven't. Why, you may be wondering. Why after all this time and when there is a guy who wants you are you still hanging onto some silly thing from the past? I don't believe that I'll meet anyone better.

I believe that whoever I try to get with, I'll be settling. That thought alone stops me.

I hug Charles, at least thankful he heard me and didn't judge me. Tears roll down my face as I feel comforted yet suffocated by Charles' embrace. I try to hide the sniffle, but Charles hears it and breaks the hug to look at me. He holds my face in his hands and wipes my tears. It's obvious I'm not trying to talk anymore so instead he talks, or should I say his lips do when they meet mine. The kiss is soft. I can tell he's trying to be gentle with me. When it ends, he hugs me again and I just quietly sob.

Chapter 25

It's crazy to think the first quarter of school is already starting to come to an end. Ten weeks flies by when you're in the hustle and bustle of things. After every quarter we have a weeklong break, and everyone gets to go home. This first quarter ends the week before Thanksgiving, so we'll get to be home for that holiday, thank God! Ten weeks is the longest I've been away from home and I'm kind of excited to go back. This school and the people in it are surprisingly starting to grow on me (I never thought I'd be saying that when I first arrived).

After the night Charles and I talked, I decided to put all of my thoughts and emotions on the back burner. With my first set of college finals around the corner, I can't afford to get distracted.

Kay and I have been studying nonstop, looking at the review packets that we received in class, the review packets from the study hub, the review outlines we made ourselves. Every now and then Charles has tried to pop into our study sessions, but I've kicked him out multiple times. He wants to express himself all the time (aka be all over me) and I'm not having it right now. Every now and then Elishea will stop by when we want a study break, or we will go to the cafeteria where she's working and just bother her for a bit. The three of us have really hit it off.

It's a fine Saturday morning and I decide to call my mom and tell her about my friends. She reminds me of date of my plane ticket, yet again.

"I hope you have it written down. And how are you getting to the airport again?"

"Mom, I told you already. The airport is on the way back home for Kay so she's just going to drop me off. Did you even hear what I said about Elishea?"

"Yes I did! I'm just glad you have girls to talk to since you barely talk to me."

"I know and I'm sorry," I say as I write "packing" on my to-do list for finals next week. "It's just been so crazy, Mom. There's constantly homework and stuff going on. Sometimes I feel like I don't even have time for myself!"

"Well, time for yourself is important. I am very excited to see you next week though! When you come, I don't know if I will want to give you any time to yourself. This is the longest you have been away from me and I miss my girl."

"I miss you, too, Mom, really. I miss everyone and I think it'll be nice to have a week to relax before starting the next quarter. Also, I have made a mental decision to be better about calling next quarter. Maybe we can schedule a time, like a least once every week on Sundays and then of course throughout the week whenever?"

"Of course. Joseph and I are always here. You know he mentioned to me the other day that he misses you, too. The house is definitely different with you being gone. Your brother is always in his room playing video games, as usual, but Joseph has been good with him. He's been taking him out, getting him to try different things in school. You know he joined the debate team?"

"Are you serious? My brother?"

"Yes, I am! He actually seems to really like it, too. It is outside of his comfort zone, but I have seen him open up a bit more and I am so proud of him."

Wow, if I didn't believe in miracles before, I surely would now. My brother kept to himself, like all the time.

Occasionally he'd talk to give some attitude, but besides that, nothing. I'm not complaining though. I'm all for change.

"Hey, Mom, does Cassidy's family still live in the area? I was thinking about visiting them. I feel like it's been such a long time!"

Cassidy was one of my, if not my only, best friends in high school. But when you live so many hours away it gets hard to keep in touch. I've reached out to Cassidy a few times and we've talked a bit, but it would be nice to actually talk in person and really catch up.

"I believe they do. You know, it's funny you bring her up because I ran into her mom at the grocery store the other day."

"Oh, really? Maybe it's a sign or something," I jokingly say.

"Maybe it is," mom replies. "Well, I'm going to let you go. I know you have plenty to prepare for with finals and I would like to get breakfast going. I love you and I will talk to you soon."

"I love you, too, Mom." We end the call and I let out a deep breath, remembering how good it always was to just talk to my mom. I'm going to be better about our relationship.

Speaking of relationships, Charles was supposed to come over this morning so he and I could study together. The past few days I've been dismissing him a lot and I think he's starting to really get upset about it. At first when I told him I wanted space to study he was like, "Of course! I don't want to be a distraction!" After like five days of that, he began asking me, "I'm guessing you're wanting space again?" I know five days isn't that long, but I guess it bothers him because we only like five minutes away from each other, since we both live on campus. Hopefully this study session is actually productive.

"Victory?" I hear a slight knock on my door.

"Come in." My roommate spent the night at her new boyfriend's room, so we have the room to ourselves.

Charles places his stuff at my desk and comes to hug me. He plants a kiss on my cheek and tries to let go, but I hold on a little longer. "I'm sorry for the way I've been acting. I've had a lot on my mind, with finals of course, the talk we had the other day, and now going back home. Instead of dealing with everything or talking about how overwhelmed I was feeling, I took it out on you, and you didn't deserve that. I'm sorry."

"It's fine. I'm not going to lie, I was starting to get frustrated, but was trying to be understanding because of finals. Do you want to talk about why going home is overwhelming you?"

He and I both know what type of response that question is going to yield and I don't have time to deal with those emotions. I need to get some studying done.

"Maybe we can talk about it later. Let's just focus on our work right now. So, physics. You want to remind me of the relationship between displacement, velocity, and acceleration?"

Charles and I bust out laughing and then dive into our work.

By the time the evening rolls around, we have thoroughly reviewed physics for four hours, dabbled into the world of calculus for another three, and played two ping-pong tournaments that resulted in serious frustration. Yes, I was the one getting frustrated. Yes, I stopped being petty and let the frustration go even after losing EVERY single game. It took some prayer, though, not gonna lie.

We decide to completely stop studying for the day and just relax. Charles puts on a football game and I try to get into it. It's funny because when I first met Charles, I really thought he was just this super nerd who only focused on school. All of that is true, however, there's more to him than that. He's funny, but sensitive, and he cares a lot. He's into other things outside of school, believe it or not. I also feel like I can talk to him about anything, although a lot of times he has to pry it out of me. Even though I still have a lot of doubts about things working out, I decide to just enjoy the rest of the evening with him. It's been a good day.

"Charles!" I yell. He jumps, obviously startled. "You know what would make this day even better? Ice cream." He stares at me, stunned.

"Okay, but did you have to yell? I'm literally right here."

"I had to yell because it's important and I want your attention. I want ice cream. Can we get the Oreo cookie dough one you, Kay and I got that one time in the beginning of the year? I'm really craving it now."

He's gathered his composure and is even kind of chuckling to himself.

"You are very extra, you know that? Sure, we can go." Thank God! Luckily, it's halftime when my craving manifests, so we're able to get the goods and be back in time to watch the second half. I'm silent during the second half, letting him have his time while I enjoy my ice cream. Every now and then I make a comment when clearly a nice play has occurred, you know to seem somewhat entertained.

It's the first day in a long time Charles and I spend together just the two of us. Kay and Elishea had texted me in the morning, but I told them we could hang out tomorrow after church or something (plot twist, Elishea also goes to the same church as us. What a God thing!) I'm thinking about Charles, church tomorrow, finals on Monday, being home on Friday, and much more when I realize I'm being tucked into my bed. The TV is turned off and my ice cream has been moved to the refrigerator. I guess I was dozing off without even realizing it.

"Good night, Victory," Charles says. I barely utter a good night and shoot up a quick prayer to God before falling into a deep sleep.

Chapter 26

Finals week has finally begun. People are walking around in their pajamas, looking like they just rolled out of bed. Others, on the other hand, use this extra time to really get made up. Like the whole look. Full faces, their best outfits on, ready to take these finals. I guess the saying look good feel good really holds true for them. I just default to leggings and a big, comfortable shirt.

I have only two finals, one in physics and one in calculus. The calc final is tonight at six and the physics final is tomorrow afternoon at one. After that, I'm done with my first quarter! I'm so excited! It's crazy to think that this Friday I'll be back home with my family. I could've returned earlier, but the airline my mom likes to use has limited flights and they're usually on Fridays. It's okay though because Tuesday evening after my last final, Kay, Elishea and I are having our final girl's night. I also think Kay is staying until Thursday to pack up the rest of her stuff, so she'll still be around. There's so much to look forward to right now, but I just got to get through the next two days.

I'm doing some last-minute reviewing before taking a long nap because I really want to be well rested for my calc exam. After a few more practice problems, I call it a day and get into bed. I'm about to close my eyes when my phone starts vibrating. Who is calling me right now? Oh, it's Charles.

"Hello?"

"Hey, Victory. What are you up to?"

"I just got done studying for the calc final. I think I'm just going to relax until dinner, that way I'm well rested. What are you up to?"

"I was just taking a break before I continued studying again. It's kind of nice not having a final until tomorrow afternoon."

"We get it. You're super smart and super ahead and came in with a million and one credits."

"You came in with a million credits yourself. I don't know what you are complaining about, babe."

"Whatever. Anyways, what's going on?"

"Nothing, I just miss you. Can I come visit you for a little bit?"

I start thinking about the amazing nap I was about to have but put it on the back burner.

"Yeah, of course." The instant I get off the phone though, I feel the sleep getting to me. I try to fight it but only stay awake for like five minutes before falling asleep. God, why is my bed so comfortable? After a while, I hear my room door open, but my eyes stay closed. It's probably just Charles. I feel him get in the bed and lay on top of the blanket I'm under. He's just places an arm around me, not realizing that I'm up.

"What time is it, Charles?"

"Oh, you're awake? It's about three. You still have plenty of time to rest. I'm guessing you set your alarm for 4:30 pm?"

"Yeah, I did. Can you wake me up then?"

"Of course." I know he doesn't like it when I turn away from him, but I actually want to sleep. He puts his head into my neck, and I know he wants me to turn toward him.

"Charles, I really want to sleep."

"I know, I just really miss you."

I face him and we start kissing. I didn't really want to, but I know that's what he wants and they always say you're supposed to compromise in a relationship, right? His hands just rest at my hips, but I still am not feeling it. I turn away from him and actually try to sleep.

"What's up, Victory?"

"I really need to sleep before this final. I want to feel well rested."

"Are you being honest with me? I don't feel like you are."

I don't want to have this conversation with Charles right now because I don't even know where to begin. I'm just not feeling it right now. This. Him.

"Really, I'm fine. Can I just have some time to myself, please?" I see Charles gets a little down, but nonetheless respects my wishes. He kisses me on the cheek before leaving. The instant he's gone, my eyes close and I am knocked out.

Chapter 27

"Hey, Elisha!" She's the first person I call after getting out of the final. I'm feeling drained, but so thankful that the first one is done.

"Hey, girl, how was your test?"

"It went well enough, but, man, four hours? That's way too long for any test!"

"I can only imagine. So, what are you up to for the rest of the night, studying?"

"I thought about it, but I don't think I can muster up any strength for that. I'm just walking back to my room now."

It's pretty cold at ten. Yeah, that's when my final got out. It's still crazy that I sat down in a room for four hours to take a test, but I guess that's my new norm for the next few years.

"Hey Elisha, do you have a few minutes for me? I want to talk to you about something." I'm kind of nervous but I need to vent about Charles to someone. Something's not quite right, but maybe I'm just being delusional. I would call Kay, but she told me she was going to sleep early tonight since she has an eight o'clock exam in the morning.

"I always have time for you. What's up?"

"I know you've been dating your boyfriend for like five years, so I guess I'm just looking for some relationship advice. Things with Charles have been, interesting? I mean everything is fine on his end, but actually really hard for me. There are so many things I'm still trying to work through that I feel like I can't give any energy to the relationship.

"He, on the other hand, seems to be committing so much time and energy to our relationship and I can't match it. There are times when he's around and I don't want him to be because I just want to be alone. When I tell him I want space though, he listens but I can tell he gets hurt. He already told me he loved me and we've only known each other for like two months? Throughout this whole thing he's been so sure, so ready, so passionate and I just want time to process it all and really get to know him. I thought I'd have this time once we started dating, but things are happening faster than I expected and am ready for."

"Wow, how long have you been feeling this way?"

"For a few weeks. I thought maybe it was me being extra because this is my first relationship, but these feelings aren't going away. I'm not sure how much longer I can handle all this."

"Have you tried talking to him about it?"

I'm back at my room and thankfully my roommate is gone, probably at her boyfriend's room. I set my backpack down and change while continuing with Elisha.

"I mean a couple of times. Earlier today he asked me what was up, but I didn't know how to say it and I wanted to chill before my final. I don't want him to think he can't express himself towards me because I'm not at the same level as him, but at the same time it's just a lot to commit to right now with everything else going on in my life. And he actually knows about the stuff from back home now, which is good."

"I mean that's definitely a good thing. Transparency and honesty are super important, and I think that you have to explain things, the way you just did with me, to him. Do you still want to be with him?"

"That's the thing. I don't know. Is it even fair to be with someone if you're not sure that's what you want?"

"That's a tough question and I guess it depends on the couple. If he knows that's where you're at and he's okay with that, then I don't see a problem. If he doesn't know though and he thinks you are as committed as he is, then that becomes an issue because you haven't been honest with him."

What she's saying completely makes sense. I think Charles and I need to talk soon because I don't want him to feel like he's being played. Obviously tonight is not a good night, but he's staying on campus through the weekend to help one of our friends from the church move into his new house. Since my flight is Friday evening, maybe Friday morning?

"Hello? Victory?"

"I'm sorry, I started thinking about when to talk to Charles. You're right, though. I really need to talk to him."

"It better not be tomorrow evening, though. I'm looking forward to us girls having our time!"

"Same girl! Hey, I'm about to sleep, but thanks for hearing me out and giving me good advice. I really appreciate it!"

"Of course! Don't forget to pray about it, too. You guys are both Christian and if you guys really want to make it work, prayer should be the foundation of y'all's relationship."

Charles and I are Christian, but we don't pray together that much. This entire quarter my relationship with God has been off because I've allowed so many other things become priorities. There are so many things I need to rethink, including my relationship with Charles. *God, may you help me get my priorities straight?*

Chapter 28

Tuesday morning, the day of my last final. Last night, even though I wanted to go to sleep early, I found myself tossing and turning a bit before shutting my eyes. I was thinking about everything: my final, Charles, my relationship with God, going home and dealing with Joseph. It's all been weighing on me. I haven't gone to the UNASHAMED Bible study in weeks and my mornings have been filled with my own personal thoughts instead of hearing God's. I've had this Bible app on my phone for forever but haven't really made too much use of it. I find a devotional on anxiety that seems interesting. I notice this specific devotional was written by a pastor my mom used to listen to a while ago. When you choose a devotional in the app, there are assigned scriptures for each day that you can read. There is also an interpretation of the scriptures and how they relate to the theme of the chosen devotional. I dive into the interpretation of the scriptures after skimming through the verses.

"Faith activates and gets God's attention, but the opposite of faith is fear which is also an activator," the devotional says. "Both activators can't coexist in the same body or else it will lead to double mindedness. Which activator is more prevalent in your life?"

If I'm honest, I have been lacking faith in basically every area of my life. I don't believe that I'll ever truly get over Joseph, I don't believe God has really been looking out for me, and I don't think life will ever get better. I feel like I'll just learn how to coast through. That's how it seems a lot of people get through life anyways, so I'm sure I could handle it. But I also don't want to just coast through. You know, when I was younger, I always imagined myself being this independent, joyful, confident resilient person who was always just killing the game, being the best at everything I did. When did that vision die? Is it even possible to still be that person? Probably not. But then another thought runs through my mind, or maybe it's the Holy Spirit. *What's the real issue?*

The million-dollar question.

God, I believe the issue is I'm trying to fill all the voids in my heart with other stuff when really, You're the only one that can fill me up. I mean I think about how things were between us before I came to college and yes, I was still struggling, but You had my back. We talked about everything all the time. There was joy that came from inside of me that life events never diminished. Now we don't even really talk, and it's taken a toll on me.

Also, I'm in this relationship and I never even talked to You about being in it. I'm running from my emotions with Joseph when I should be addressing and working through them. I'll admit that Kay and Elisha have been huge blessings and I know You brought them in my life so I could still hear from You even though I wasn't investing much into us. Thank You for still watching out for me like that.

What I really need Father is Your help. I'm sorry for putting stress, worry, and everything else above my relationship with You. I've been activating fear for way too long. May we do a little exchange? If I give You my fears about whether I should be in this relationship with Charles, my fears about going home and facing Joseph, and my fears about being too broken to enjoy a happy life, will You bless me with a new seed of faith? From there, by reading Your word and investing in us more, the faith can grow into something bigger. I know that faith is a foundational aspect of the Christian walk because without it, there's literally no belief. Help my unbelief Father. And thank You for giving me this time to talk to You.

As I leave my quiet time to have lunch before my the final, I feel different. A little freer than before. A part of me wonders how things could've been better this past quarter if I had been more consistent with my relationship with God. Maybe I would've felt this free the whole time. Maybe I'd be stronger emotionally and mentally. Maybe I wouldn't be in a relationship.-

Although these last ten weeks didn't go as I thought they would, I've still learned a lot. And to be honest, I also ended up enjoying college more than I expected to. I have a better head on my shoulders moving forward, for which I can only be thankful to God. Maybe moving forward I will feel free all the time, even as I work through my struggles. Maybe I will open up to my mom about everything, considering she already knows and still loves me anyways. Maybe I will become that resilient person I've always wanted to be. Maybe I will live up to my name and finally achieve victory for myself.

About the Author

Originally born in Nouak-chott, Mauritania, Mary-Helen Victoria Shomba grew up in Round Rock, Texas with her parents and three siblings. Victoria is a recent graduate from Rose-Hulman Institute of Technology with a Bachelor of Science in Mechanical Engineering  and a minor in Entrepreneurship. Despite this technical background, Victoria has a passion for art, writing, and music, as she draws, reads, makes beats, raps, and sings in her free time. *Victory* is Victoria's first book!